(megan) 2

MARY HOOPER

BLOOMSBURY

First published in Great Britain in 1999
Bloomsbury Publishing Plc, 38 Soho Square, London, W1V 5DF

Copyright © Mary Hooper 1999

The moral right of the author has been asserted
A CIP catalogue record of this book is available from the
British Library

ISBN 0 7475 4169 8

Printed in Great Britain by Clays Ltd, St Ives plc

10 9 8 7 6 5 4 3 2

Gemma
Second baby
Never second best

CHAPTER ONE

When I woke up properly it was day. The hospital ward was hot and bright with sunshine, and along my back I was wet with sweat from the plastic mattress underneath me.

I still didn't feel that things were real. Surely it wasn't true. Surely I hadn't had a baby. How *could* I have? Having babies was a grown-up sort of thing; a married and mortgage thing that friends' older sisters and aunties did. How had I managed to have a baby?

I'd had the weirdest night ever. I'd woken on and off and heard babies crying somewhere in the distance, and people talking and laughing, and then someone rattling a trolley around. In-between this I'd slept and had funny dreams: one where I'd gone out with the baby and had left him on a bus, and a strange one in which he'd grown enormous overnight, so that I couldn't get him through the front door at home. In the worst, most nightmarish one, Mum had come to hospital to collect me, but we hadn't taken the baby.

We'd just pushed him into a dark corner and abandoned him.

Remembering the dream again and feeling a sudden panic, I struggled to sit up. There was no cot beside my bed now, but there had been, sometime earlier, and I could dimly remember a nurse telling me that she was taking the baby into a nursery for the night to make sure that I got a good night's sleep.

I wasn't quite sure how long I'd been on this ward; exactly when I'd arrived. I knew I'd come from the operating theatre, where I'd had a Caesarean, some time yesterday, but whether it had been daytime when I'd arrived, or the evening, or the middle of the night, I couldn't remember. I knew that Mum had come in to see me, but I'd been too exhausted and woozy from the operation to talk to her much, and I couldn't remember her going home, so I think I must have fallen asleep in the middle of her visit.

I tugged at the curtain which divided me from the rest of the ward, trying to pull it back and see round it. There were three other screened-off beds in the room, and on the far side was a glass dividing wall with a hallway along which nurses were coming and going. On the other side of this hallway was the nursery, and I could just see the tops of some plastic cots.

Was that where my baby was?

'Ow!' I'd tried to move again and with the effort had pulled at the stitches that held my tummy together. I put my hand under my nightie and onto the gauze covering and tried to count how many there were. Six, was it? Or maybe eight.

I flopped down again and lay still for some moments, feeling again the panic that had accompanied the dreams. In that nursery, just over the way, was a baby. *My own baby*. It was a boy and he was entirely my responsibility. I had to look after him, feed, clothe and care for him and take him everywhere with me forever. Or not quite forever, but near enough.

And I hadn't even told Mum that I wanted to keep him yet.

Suppose she wouldn't let me? Suppose he was taken away from me? Or suppose they didn't take him away, but I had nowhere to go with him and was homeless, left wandering round the streets?

I began to breathe in sharp, shallow pants, feeling almost faint: *What was going to happen to me and the baby?*

'Morning!' A blue-uniformed nurse came in and zipped down the centre of the ward, pulling all the bed-curtains open as she went. 'Here come the babies!'

As I tried again to sit up, another nurse came in, pushing two see-through cots in front of her.

'Baby Boyle and Baby Warrell,' she announced.

'Baby Warrell's mine,' I said, hearing the uncertainty in my voice and feeling sure she was going to say, 'Don't be ridiculous. Of course it's not *your* baby.'

She didn't, though. She pushed the cot right up to the top of my bed. The baby inside it, my baby, was tightly wrapped in a white cotton blanket that went right over his head, leaving just his small pink face showing.

I gave a gasp of surprise and delight. There he was. There he really was.

'Breast or bottle-feeding?' the nurse asked me.

I hardly heard her, I was too busy staring.

'Breast or bottle?' she said again.

'Bottle,' I said. It seemed easier, somehow. Less shameful. I'd always been mortally embarrassed at anyone breast-feeding in front of me.

She delivered the other baby to the bed on my left, and then came back to me.

I was still staring down into the cot. The baby was lying peacefully, the blanket cocooned around him. I didn't want to disturb him. And I wasn't sure how to pick him up, either.

'Aren't you getting him up?' the nurse asked.

'He looks so peaceful,' I said. And so fragile, too. A tiny, pink china object that might break if handled wrongly.

'He wasn't peaceful in the night,' said the nurse. 'Little monkey! Two feeds since midnight, he's had.'

I leaned forward awkwardly in the bed to try and reach him, and gasped as my stitches pulled. I wished the nurse would go away so that I could work out how to handle him. I wasn't sure which bit to go for: should I sort of drag him out from the top, or go underneath and scoop?

'Mind your stitches,' the nurse said. 'I'll get him up for you, shall I?'

She bent over the cot, lifted the baby up effortlessly and laid him in my arms. 'Look at you!' she said, smiling. 'Anyone would think you'd never held a baby before!'

I swallowed. 'I . . . '

'It's okay,' she said, patting my hand. 'We all have to learn. I'll be back in a minute to show you how to feed him.'

She went out again and carefully I unwrapped the top of the blanket bundle and stroked his dark hair.

He was truly beautiful. His skin was pink and

gleaming, his cheeks were round, his eyelashes were long and his nose was the tiniest little piggy thing I'd ever seen. He was wearing a grey-coloured hospital nightie, creased and shapeless, and out of the sleeves of this stuck small pink hands, splayed like starfish. I opened the blanket further and lifted the nightdress to see plump, ringed ankles and red feet with ridiculously small toes, complete with nails. The smallest toe had a silvery nail as tiny as a pin-head.

I giggled with delight. He was perfect. Entirely, absolutely perfect.

'Where did you come from?' I asked him. How could it be that Megan Warrell, immensely average until she'd got pregnant at fifteen and been hounded out of school, had managed to have this perfect angel baby?

The nurse came back carrying a small bottle of milk, and I started guiltily and began to wrap him up again.

'That's okay!' she said. 'That's what you're supposed to do. He's your baby. You must play with him and talk to him and love him as much as you can.'

I looked at her, blinked, and burst into tears.

'That's okay, too,' she said, patting my hand.

I slept again after lunch. Well, they called it lunch: it was a sandwich and a rice pudding. While we slept they took the babies back into the nursery, so that we wouldn't be disturbed. We were disturbed, though: two of the four girls in my room went home, and one new one arrived. I was the only long stay, being a Caesarean.

That morning I'd learned how to give a bottle of milk and get a baby's wind up, and how to clean a bottom and change a nappy. Tomorrow, when I could move around better, I was going to be shown how to bath and top-and-tail. I'd seen some of these things done when I'd been staying at Auntie Lorna's and going to the educational unit, but it was all different now with my own baby. I had to do it absolutely right. I didn't want anyone to think that just because I was only fifteen I couldn't handle him.

I'd started to think about names. I hadn't bothered before because I didn't know whether I'd be keeping him and also because, deep down, I didn't really believe that I was having a baby at all. Now I thought about Ben, and Zak, and Josh. And then I thought maybe something a bit more fancy: Elliot or Russell or Dermot.

That morning, I'd spoken quite a lot to the nicest

nurse, whose name was Debs, and confessed that I'd only just made up my mind to keep the baby when I'd actually had him. She'd told me that hardly any unmarried girls gave their babies up now, that the girls' parents nearly always allowed them to bring their babies home.

'I'm sure your mum will be okay,' she'd said.

I'd sighed. 'Doubt it. You don't know what she's like. She's one of those women who're always worried about what the neighbours will say.'

'Once she sees him properly she'll give in. He's her grandchild, after all.'

'I know that,' I'd said, biting my lip, 'but she goes on and on about me getting my A Levels and going to university and getting a good job and all that.' I'd looked down at the baby in my arms. 'Things like that don't matter compared to him, though, do they?'

Debs had pulled a face. 'Well, they *do* matter,' she'd said. 'You won't want to stay home looking after that baby for the rest of your life, you know.'

'Well,' I'd said, shrugging, 'I'll go to night school or whatever and get some qualifications.'

I'd said it flippantly, but the thought caught hold of me: what was I going to do with my life? Could I go to evening classes? Could I still, somehow take exams? *How* could I?

I think I only slept for a while, and when I woke up the new girl in my ward had a toddler jumping on her bed and a man – her husband, I supposed – was standing by her side with a big bunch of flowers. This made me think about Luke, my ex-boyfriend and the baby's father, and I wondered whether he knew yet and whether he'd visit me. Would my friends come? Did Dad know yet? He was divorced from my mum and lived in Australia with his new family, but Mum had said she'd ring him.

I felt a bit stronger about things; better than I had done first thing that morning. Before I did anything else, though, I had to tell Mum that I wasn't giving up the baby. According to what she said, I would then decide what to do. If she wouldn't have us at home, then we'd have to find somewhere else to live. I'd get in touch with Susie, my social worker, and she'd have to find me a hostel, or a bed and breakfast place. They weren't that awful, surely?

I heard Debs's voice from the hallway.

'Megan's absolutely fine, Mrs Warrell,' she was saying. 'And the baby's in the nursery at the moment. Do you want to see him first?'

'I'll go and see my daughter, thanks,' I heard Mum

15

say. She had her posh voice on.

I squirmed back under the bedclothes a little. Deciding to tell Mum I was keeping the baby was one thing, doing it was another. I closed my eyes, pretending to sleep, putting off the moment for a few seconds more.

Mum bent and kissed me. 'You awake? Are you all right, love?' she asked.

I opened my eyes and nodded slightly. 'Yes, thanks. Just tired.'

She looked over to the nursery. 'I'm surprised the baby is down here with you.'

'What d'you mean?'

'I thought when babies were being adopted they kept them apart from their mums. They asked me if I wanted to see him and I thought it best not to.'

I didn't say anything.

She laid a bunch of flowers on the bed. 'I'm so relieved you're all right.' She smoothed my hair in a very (for her) motherly way. 'I didn't sleep at all last night. This morning I rang Auntie Lorna – and your dad. Woke him up, actually; it was four in the morning there.'

I smiled. 'What did he say?'

'He sent his love and said he's writing. He said I'm

16

to take you on holiday and get you back on your feet – he's got some business deal coming up so he's going to send us some money.' She tucked a strand of hair behind my ears. 'That's the ticket, eh? Get us all back to normal.'

I swallowed. 'Well . . . ' I began.

'And it's about time he coughed up something!'

'I want to . . . '

She patted my hand. 'I know it's going to be difficult for you, love, but least said soonest mended and all that. We'll sign all the papers and get you out of here, and then we'll have a good holiday. After that you can think about starting an A Level course. You might not want to go back to that school – it's up to you.'

I drew in my breath to speak but she started again, hardly pausing between sentences.

'Ellie wanted to visit but I thought it might be unsettling for her. I didn't want her to see the baby and get upset about it.' She picked up the flowers. 'Shall I get a vase for these? Will the nurses have one out there?'

'I expect so,' I said. I felt too weak; I couldn't think about starting an argument.

'Your Auntie Lorna said she'd try and get to see

17

you before she goes to Italy – did you know she's got a three-month job up in the mountains there? She's very pleased you're all right. Now, what d'you want me to do about ringing your friends? If you don't want me to ring I think there's a phone in here you can use and if I get you a phonecard . . . '

She went on nineteen to the dozen, from one subject to the next, as if she was scared to let me get in between her sentences. I let her words rattle on, wondering how I was going to get round to saying what I had to. And then something happened . . .

'Here come the babies!' Debs called, and she came through from the nursery pushing a cot with him – my baby – inside. Mum turned round in alarm as Debs stopped at the end of the bed. 'Here's your lovely grandson, Mrs Warrell!' she said, winking slightly at me.

'Oh, but I didn't . . . we're not . . . ' Mum began.

'He's gorgeous! D'you want to hold him?' Debs said, and before Mum could protest she'd picked him up and placed him in her arms.

Mum looked down at him, startled, as if he was an alien life form, and for a moment it looked as if she was going to thrust him back at Debs. Then, as I held my breath and watched, she put out a hand and stroked his cheek. Then she put her finger into his hand so that he grasped it.

She was quiet for a long time, just looking at him. Then she broke the silence. 'Incredible. He looks just like you did. It brings it all back.'

I swallowed. 'I don't want to give him up, Mum,' I said. 'I don't want him adopted. I can't bear to give him away, I really can't.'

There was an even longer silence, and then Mum said, 'No. Of course you can't. I pretended you'd be able to, but I was only kidding myself.' She shook her head wearily. 'Oh well, we'll just have to try and sort something out, won't we? I don't know what, but I daresay I'll think of something.'

Ward 7
St Brides' General Hospital

August 10*th*

Dear Dad (and Grandad!)

Just a short note. I'm too shattered to write much, but too churned-up to sleep. I know Mum has rung you already, and thanks in advance for the holiday money. I'm not sure if we'll be going on holiday, though, because I'm writing to say that I'm keeping the baby! He's just gorgeous and I love him to bits. I couldn't possibly let him go.

Mum is being okay about it. I'm so excited but I'm going to try and sleep now.

Lots of love, Megan

CHAPTER TWO

The baby was three days old before anyone other than Mum and Ellie came to see us. I'd rung Susie by then and told her I was definitely keeping him, and she'd promised to come in and see us as soon as she could. I knew that, having had a Caesarean, I wouldn't be going home for a while.

Home. I was dying to get home. I wanted my baby all to myself, to show him off to my friends and to take him out places. I had to decide on a name (I was thinking of Ronan, Aidan and Marc at the moment) and I knew I had to try and sort out what my life was going to be like. I was scared about all sorts of things: about seeing people – especially the boys at school who'd been horrible to me – and about looking after a baby, and about what was going to happen with boyfriends now and all that sort of stuff, but I wanted to get on with it. I'd been on the sidelines for months; being pushed about, having to do what everyone else thought I should do. Now I wanted to get moving again. It was ages since I'd gone out doing normal things with my mates. *Years.*

Luke appeared in the ward when I was giving the baby a bottle. I saw him outside, looking awkward and out of place, and had time to open my locker and run a brush through my hair before he came in. Well, I might not fancy him any more, but I didn't want him to think that I was letting myself go.

A nurse pointed him to where I was, and he came in and just stood there in front of the bed looking really embarrassed, holding a blue basket of flowers shaped like a cradle.

'Hello!' I said. 'How are you? Want to hold the baby?'

'No, no!' he said hastily. He stared at the baby as if hypnotised, moving closer to the bed all the time.

'Sit down,' I said. He looked quite nice, actually. Quite fanciable. His hair had grown long and was blond at the front and he had new glasses.

'What . . . how are you?' he said, still staring at the baby.

'Fine!' I said airily. I really was feeling better every day, and could move around quite easily now. On the doctors' round that morning they'd said I was making remarkable progress.

I finished feeding the baby and sat him on my lap to get his wind up. I was showing off a bit, I suppose. Showing Luke how good a mum I was.

'Who told you I'd had him?' I asked. 'Don't say Mum rang!'

He shook his head. 'Your mum rang Claire and she told me. I saw her and Josie in town this morning.'

'Is Claire coming in to see me?' I asked, wondering why my best friend, of all people, hadn't been in already.

'She was coming tonight,' he said. 'But I said I ought to go first. I think she's coming tomorrow.' He put out a tentative hand towards the baby but didn't quite reach him. 'A boy, eh? What are you going to call him?'

'Can't decide,' I said. 'You know my friend Amy – the girl I met when I was at that educational unit? – well, she had a boy the same day as me and she's calling him Meredith. Bit of a weird choice but it's her boyfriend's middle name. She sent a card saying she was at home already. She had a normal birth, see.'

'Oh,' he said, but he didn't ask what wasn't normal about mine.

I nodded towards the blue basket he was still carrying. 'Are those flowers for me?'

Suddenly seeming to remember what he was holding, he dumped the basket on the bed. 'Yeah. Congratulations.'

'Congratulations to you,' I said. 'Well, *you're* the dad.'

'Are you really keeping him?'

I nodded violently.

'Claire said you were.' He shook his head. 'How will you manage, though?'

I shrugged. 'Dunno. I just can't give him away, that's all.'

He coughed. 'I got my results today.'

'Your A Levels! I forgot,' I said. 'How did you get on?'

'Two Bs and a C. I've got into Sheffield.'

'Fantastic!'

The baby gave a small burp.

'Is that all right?' Luke asked anxiously, studying the baby's face.

'Course it is!' I laid the baby on the bed face down, and rubbed his back. 'That's just a bit of wind.'

'What are you going to call him?'

I sighed. 'I don't know. I keep thinking of all sorts of names, but none are exactly right. Got any ideas?'

Luke shook his head, staring at the baby as if it was

going to jump off the bed and bite him.

'How are your mum and dad?'

'About *him?*' He pulled a face. 'They read me the riot act when they found out – when you and your mum came round that time – but over the weeks it's all died down.'

'Do they know I've had him?'

He shook his head again. 'Don't think so. All they've been on about lately is my results. And going to Sheffield.'

He put out his hand and touched the baby's head. 'He's nice, isn't he?'

'Nice?!' I said. 'He's gorgeous. The most gorgeous creature in the world.'

'Okay,' he laughed.

'Hold him,' I urged. 'Have a cuddle.' I picked up the baby and placed him in Luke's arms. 'There you go!'

He held the baby awkwardly, stiffly, at arm's length.

'Cuddle him,' I urged.

He tried. He did his best, but he still looked as if he was cuddling a log.

'When you go away . . . when you go to Sheffield, will you keep in touch with us?' I asked.

'Of course!' He looked shocked. 'Of course I will. I'll send him things.'

'You say that now . . . '

He stared down at the baby, stared for ages. 'Fancy,' he said. 'A baby.'

I didn't say anything.

'Suppose,' he went on after a long moment, 'I didn't go to Sheffield after all.'

'What d'you mean?'

'Suppose I stayed here and got a job.'

I was amazed. 'Then what?'

'Suppose I stayed and looked after you both. We could be together and bring him up between us. We could get married later on.'

'Oh,' I said, and my heart was pumping so that I could almost hear it. Was this what I wanted? This could . . . just . . . be the answer. I needn't go back to Mum, who was bound to be bossy and try and take over. Luke and I could bring up the baby on our own, be a real family.

The baby let out a cry and Luke hastily passed him back to me. I cuddled him in my arms, seeing me and Luke in one of those sofa advertisements, curled up in front of the fire together, laughing, the baby between us.

'I didn't expect a marriage proposal,' I said, giggling nervously. 'And me in my nightie and all.'

'We needn't get married yet,' he said, hastily, 'but we could get a flat together. I'll help you with the baby and we'll get married when it's a year old and it can come and watch.'

'What would your mum and dad say? They wouldn't let you.'

'They wouldn't be able to stop me. How could they?'

I shrugged. The pictures persisted: I could see us shopping together, and on picnics, and building sand-castles at the seaside. I could see us going for a walk with the baby in a carrier on Luke's shoulders.

'I mean, we get on, don't we?' he said.

I nodded.

'So what's to stop us? Your mum will be pleased, won't she?'

'I 'spose so.'

'It's what she wanted – for me to marry you. And I can help you with the baby and everything. It'd be great! We can have our mates round whenever we want – have parties! I'll get a job at the printers or some-where and we'll get our names on the council list.'

I nodded slowly. It sounded okay. It seemed the right thing to do. The baby would have a father, his proper father, and I'd have someone around all the time to give me a hand and to help pay for things. And I wouldn't have to worry about what people said about me any more; I'd be a young married mum, instead of an unmarried one. Boys wouldn't be able to shout at me in the street; Luke would be there to stop them.

'Where would we live, though?' I asked.

'We'd rent a flat! I'll get the newspaper on the way home and see how much they are.'

I rocked the baby gently. It seemed best for him, and best for me. 'All right, then,' I said slowly. 'But I'd have to go home with my mum from here. I couldn't move in with you just like that.'

'Yeah, well I doubt if I can find a flat that quickly, anyway.'

'And I haven't got anything ready. Not even a nappy. There's a load of things I've got to buy.'

'I'll get some money from my dad! Because I won't be going to university we can have that money for the baby instead.' He punched the air. 'It'll be fantastic. We can have a really funky flat with all trendy furniture. And if we can't afford proper seats we can sit on deckchairs.'

I rocked the baby in my arms, suddenly tremendously excited. 'Yeah! It'll be brilliant!'

Ward 7
St Brides' General Hospital

August 12th

Dear Amy,

Hurray! It's all over. I got your card and guess what, I had my baby the same day. A boy, too, and nearly the same weight as yours! The name Meredith is really nice and unusual but I don't know what I'm calling mine yet.

I'm really excited because, guess what, my ex-boyfriend, the baby's father, just came in and said he wants us to live together and get married!

I'll write again soon.

Lots of love, Megan

CHAPTER THREE

Ward 7
St Brides' General Hospital

August 13th

Dear Susie,

I tried to ring you, but your office said you'd be out all day. I know Mum has rung you to tell you I'm keeping the baby, what I'm writing for now is to say that I might be getting married! Luke came in yesterday, and he thought the baby was fantastic. He says he's not going to university now, he wants us to get a flat together.

What do you think? I'm writing to you because I don't know what Mum will say. If I tell her that you're all for it, it might make her all for it as well.

Luke says he'll get a job and try and find us a bed-sitter or something, and we can go on the council list to get a flat and get married later. Will this be all right, do you think? I don't know what his mum and dad will say.

I hope you've got time to come in and see me and advise me! The baby is brilliant, by the way.

Love from Megan

I stuck Susie's letter in an envelope, thinking deeply. Mum hadn't come in last night, so I hadn't been able to say anything to her about Luke. And this morning I felt very weird and unsure about all the things we'd said, though I didn't know why.

As I put a stamp on the envelope, I heard a tapping on the partition.

'There she is!'

Claire and Josie were outside in the hallway, giggling and waving at me through the glass.

'Can we come in?' Claire asked, putting her head round the door.

I nodded. 'Course you can.'

I wished Claire had come on her own. The fact that they'd come in together just confirmed they were going about in a twosome all the time, that Josie had moved into the best friend slot that I'd vacated.

They stood at the bottom of my bed, still giggling.

'Where's the baby?' Claire asked in a hushed whisper.

'Here,' I pointed to the other side of my bed. 'He's fast asleep.'

They pushed each other out of the way to get to the cot first, then stood looking at him.

'Aaaah!' Claire said.

'Sweet!' Josie said, then she added, 'He doesn't look much like Luke, does he?'

'He doesn't look like anyone at the moment,' I said. I swung my legs out of the bed. 'I'll get him up so you can see him properly.'

Josie, alarmed, made a face towards the nurses outside. 'Are you allowed?'

'Course I am. He's mine!'

As I picked up the baby he gave a sleepy cry of protest, then a snuffle.

'Aaahh!' Claire said again.

Josie gave a sniggery laugh. 'Isn't he funny?' she said. 'Look at his face! They do look like little old men, don't they?'

I settled the baby in my arms. After a comment like that *she* certainly wasn't going to hold him.

'Have you got a name for him yet?' Claire asked.

'I've got loads of names,' I said. 'I can't decide. My best ones at the moment are Ryan and Lloyd.'

'I've done you a top twenty boys' names,' she said, pulling it out of her pocket.

I grinned. We always used to do top twenties in class, when the lesson got boring. We did top twenty teachers and boys and snogs-in-films and designer labels. Top twenty anythings.

'And I've got something for the baby as well,' Claire went on, handing me a paper bag. 'I've kept the receipt in case it's not right.'

I opened the bag and pulled out a tiny pair of denim jeans and a matching white T-shirt. 'Thanks a lot,' I said, meaning it. 'They're really nice. They're the first real clothes he's got.'

'Was it awful – having him?' Josie asked. 'Did it really hurt? Did you scream?'

I pulled a face. 'It wasn't too bad,' I said. 'I had a Caesarean in the end so I didn't know too much.'

'Have you got a big scar, then?'

'It's a bikini scar,' I said. 'They call it that because you can still wear one.'

'Are you . . . like . . . breast-feeding?' Josie asked in a fascinated-yet-horrified whisper.

'I put him straight on a bottle,' I said, shaking my head. 'Anyway, what *is* this, twenty questions? Why don't you tell me what's happening outside? Who've you seen? What's everyone doing? Who's got off with who?'

Josie nudged Claire. Claire nudged her back.

'We saw Luke yesterday,' Claire began tentatively.

I nodded. 'He told me. He came in last night.'

'Tell her, then,' Josie put in.

'Tell me what?'

'Claire fancies Luke like *mad*,' Josie said.

'I do not!'

'Not much you don't. Anyway, it doesn't matter, does it? Megan won't mind.' Josie appealed to me, 'You don't care, do you? You haven't been out with Luke for ages.'

'Well . . . ' I said. I felt pressured and confused. Things were all happening too fast: I'd had a baby, and thought he might be adopted, then he wasn't going to be, then I was taking him home to live with Mum, then I was getting married. I wasn't sure where I was any more.

'He's going away soon, anyway,' Josie said. 'Got in at Sheffield, didn't he?'

'Yeah, well,' I said. 'He might not be. I might be

getting back together with him.'

'*What?*' They both looked at me, startled.

'Blimey,' Josie said. 'What brought this on?'

I shrugged. 'I think it was actually seeing the baby. Luke just thought it would be nice to make a go of it now we've got him.'

'What – you might start going out with him again?' Claire asked.

'No. I mean we might start living together.' As I said it, I didn't sound like *me* saying it, I sounded like someone very grown up. 'We might get together, get married, and bring the baby up properly, as a family.'

'Gawd!' Josie said, and she looked at Claire. 'You'd better lay off him, then. You should have seen her yesterday,' she said to me, 'all over him like a rash, she was.'

'I wasn't!' Claire said hotly.

'Well, she thought he was up for grabs. It's different if you're going back with him.'

I busied myself with the baby, not knowing what to say. I couldn't be cross with Claire, because she hadn't known that Luke and I would get together again. Until yesterday I hadn't known it myself. And anyway, were we *really?*

'Nothing's settled yet,' I said.

There was an awkward silence.

'Here, wasn't it exciting when you went into labour at home?' Josie said. 'When your waters went on the carpet! I nearly died of horror. I didn't know it all happened like that.'

'No,' I said absently, trying to conjure again the image of me, Luke and the baby on the sofa.

'Gawd, we might have had to deliver that baby ourselves.' She nudged Claire. 'Think of that. All that blood and gore. You have to tie the cord, don't you? And they're always calling for hot water. Why's that?'

Claire didn't reply. She stared at the baby and said to me, 'Sorry about Luke. I mean, I didn't realise you were going to . . . '

'It's all right,' I said.

'When will you get married?' Josie asked. ''Spect your mum'll be pleased.'

I nodded. 'I expect so.'

'What?!' Mum said, exactly one hour later. 'Marry that boy? Don't be ridiculous.'

I stared at her, amazed. 'But I thought you'd be pleased! The minute I told you I was pregnant that's the first thing you said: that I'd have to get married.'

'That was in the heat of the moment. That was just the shock of it all. No, it's ridiculous. You can't possibly get married – you're only fifteen!'

'I'm sixteen next month,' I pointed out.

'Just a child yourself.'

'Luke will be able to help me with the baby.'

'Fat lot of help a boy that age will be. Besides, his parents won't let him.'

'How d'you know?'

'You said he'd got in at university. They've got *plans* for him. They won't let him throw away his chances by tying himself down and getting some dead-end job round here.'

The sofa, the seaside and the picnic all began to slip away.

'You have absolutely no idea what bringing up a baby entails. It's a bloody hard slog. You can't just play at it.'

I began to cry.

'Look, I don't want to get you upset, love, but it's really not on. It's a terrible idea. Even the best, most suitable marriages are down-right difficult, and as for this: two bits of kids bringing up a baby with no money and no prospects! Well, you stand no chance at all.'

I cried into the box of hankies she'd brought in for me.

'You don't even love Luke, do you? I don't *once* remember you telling me that you loved him.'

'I didn't think that would matter,' I sniffed.

She shook her head. 'It does matter. It would be a disaster. I can't let you go through with it.'

I sobbed louder, deeply relieved. Almost the minute Luke had gone I'd started to have doubts about going back with him, and telling Claire and Josie had just made it worse. I didn't love Luke, I probably never had done. And how would I have coped with a *husband* as well as a baby? A husband – well, you had to cook for them and iron things and clean things and I was useless at all that sort of stuff. I still wanted someone to look after *me*.

Mum looked at me. 'You knew it wasn't really on, didn't you? You just thought it might be an easy way out.'

I nodded.

'I thought so. That's why you're not arguing!'

As I blew my nose, Ellie came into view in the corridor, bent over the cot as she pushed it along. The baby had been crying so she'd taken him for a walk between the wards.

39

'He's gone to sleep!' she called from the doorway. 'Shall I bring him back in?'

I nodded and put away the tissues.

'Have you been crying?' she asked. Her little snub nose was a lot like the baby's.

'Only a bit.'

'What for?'

I shrugged.

'All new mothers cry a lot,' Mum said, patting me on the hand. 'It's the hormones.'

'When you're home can I take him for a walk every day?' Ellie asked, her face only inches away from the baby's.

'Course you can,' I said.

'I wish you'd hurry up and give him a name. I like Wayne best,' she said. 'Call him Wayne.'

'Wayne Warrell?' I shuddered. 'I think not.'

'It might be nice to call him after my father – Francis,' Mum said.

I pulled a face.

'What are you going to buy that I can walk him in?' Ellie wanted to know. 'A pram or a push-chair?'

'At the rate we're going, a crate on wheels,' Mum said. 'We can't afford anything else.'

I looked at her anxiously. I was worried about buying a

pram, and clothes for the baby, and nappies, and a cot and all the other hundred and one things I knew you needed. Mum kept talking about jumble sales and second-hand shops, but I desperately wanted beautiful *new* things for my baby. 'Susie said I'll get a grant,' I said.

'That won't get us far,' Mum said, 'but I'm working on your father.'

'When I come home, where are we all going to sleep?' I asked. 'Is Ellie going to come back into my room, or what?'

Mum raised her eyebrows. 'Oh, you're not coming home with us,' she said. 'You and the baby will be going to a foster home.'

I gasped and Ellie looked up, horrified, from the cot.

Mum laughed. 'I'm teasing you! Of course you're coming home. Don't be so daft!'

I swallowed hard. I'd nearly started crying again. Mum making a joke! I wasn't used to it.

When she'd gone I tore up the letter to Susie.

CHAPTER FOUR

Ward 7
St Brides' General Hospital

August 15th

Dear Lorna,

Thank you ever so much for the letter and the cheque. I was really excited: I've never seen a big amount like that before. I'll be able to buy loads for the baby, starting with a push-chair. You can get ones now that go into about five different things – when I was staying with you I noticed the woman next door had one.

I was supposed to be going home from the hospital today but when they took my temperature it was slightly up, so they're going to keep me in a day or so longer.

The baby is brilliant, like a little doll. I haven't

named him yet but my favourite names at the mo are Luca, Aidan or Zak. I change my mind all the time, though. As soon as I can, I'll get a photo of him to you. Don't worry about trying to get to the hospital before you go to Italy; we'll still be here (not in the hospital I don't mean) when you come back. That job sounds really exciting.

Now I've had my baby, I know just how difficult it must have been for you to give up yours. Once I'd seen him, and held him, I knew that I couldn't. No wonder that you think about your son every day. I'm glad you've registered on that list of mums who've had their babies adopted. Okay, so your son may not have put his name down on the 'babies' list yet, but he might one day. Perhaps when he's got a baby of his own he'll think of you. I'm sure he *does* think of you anyway.

Two of my mates have been in to visit me. It was nice to see them but really weird, too, because everything was so different. I felt sort-of removed from them. Much older! I wanted to hear what everyone was getting up to, all the scandal, but when they told me I just thought, *so what?*

It's funny in here, like I'm in a cocoon where nothing else matters but me and the baby. He fills every moment of the day, even when I'm not feeding or changing him I'm cuddling him or looking at him.

The other visitor I've had was Luke – the baby's father. He got a bit carried away and said we could live together and get married next year! Mum said she thought it was a ridiculous idea, though, and anyway, would you believe that I haven't heard from him since?! That's how much he meant it.

Mum brought in a card from Amy – you remember, the girl I made friends with in the Mother and Baby unit when I was staying with you. She had a boy the same day as me, almost the same weight. She's home already, because she had a normal birth. (I had my stitches out yesterday. Ow! × 7.) She is calling her baby Meredith. I think it's a really weird name, but it's her boyfriend's middle one. Talking of names, you told me once that you named your baby, but his adoptive mother gave him a different one. What was the name you gave him?

You asked me how Mum had been about me keeping him. The answer is: really good. Better than I thought she would be. She seemed to come round to the idea almost immediately. She told me that, deep down, she'd known all along that I wouldn't have him adopted, but she wanted to encourage me to do so because she thought it would be better. Don't worry, I haven't told her anything about you. I wouldn't.

Ellie really loves the baby. As soon as she gets to the hospital she picks him up and smothers him with kisses. She's okay, actually. I'm getting on with her much better now.

I've been going to mothercraft classes here: just a couple of hours where they show you the best way of bathing a baby, and different ways of putting on a nappy (in case you don't want to use disposable ones) and how to sterilise feeding bottles. It looks like a right fuss, this bottle business, you have to have a sterilising unit and loads of bottles on the go – it almost makes me wish I'd started breast feeding. Not quite, though. I'm waiting for my milk to dry up and have to wear horrible round flying saucer things in my bra until it does. Yuk.

Anyway, have a lovely time in Italy. I know you're working but I bet you find time to have some adventures as well.

Thanks once again for the money. I'm going to have a lovely spend-up and I'll let you know what I buy.

Lots of love, Megan

Carefully, clutching my tummy, I put on my dressing gown, pushed the baby back into the nursery and went downstairs, where there was a tea bar and a couple of shops, to post the letter.

As I put it in the post box, someone tapped me on the shoulder. I wheeled round and it was Izzy – a girl who'd gone to my school but, like me, had been chucked out because she was pregnant. Her baby was now a grubby toddler, and she was pregnant again and almost ready to drop. I'd bumped into her before on an ante-natal appointment.

'What did you have?' she asked.

'A boy,' I said proudly. 'He's upstairs.'

'What are you calling him?'

'Don't know yet,' I said. Since Claire had come in with her list, I had another twenty names to choose from. 'At the moment I like Stevie and Gavin. Or Gabriel.'

'*She's* called Gabriel,' she said, indicating the toddler hanging on her. 'It's a boy or girl's name, innit?'

Feeling our eyes on her, the little girl began to grizzle, pushing her face into Izzy's skirt and leaving a trail from her nose across it.

I decided I didn't like the name after all.

'How long have you got to go now?' I asked.

'Two weeks,' she said, her lip curling. 'It seems like forever with this one. The little sod doesn't give me a minute's peace: kicks me to death, he does.'

I smiled uneasily. 'I thought it was a good sign if they were active.'

'Yeah, great. It means they'll be bloody active when they're born – and I'll be climbing the bleedin' wall. Get up, Gabriel!' She made a move towards the child, who'd let go of her skirt and was lying on the floor, rolling towards what looked like a puddle of orange juice.

'What d'you do with yourself all day?' I asked. 'Do you get out much?'

'Gab!' she snapped as Gabriel reached the puddle. The toddler didn't take any notice. 'What's there to go out for?' she asked me. 'Out of the house, every-thing costs money.'

'I 'spose so,' I said.

'Has the father of your kid scarpered?'

'Not really,' I said slowly. Had he, though? I knew I ought to write to him and tell him that it – us – wasn't going to happen. I wanted to get it in before he did.

'If he hasn't scarpered yet, he will soon enough,' Izzy said sourly. 'Gabriel's father hung around about a month, but this-one-in-here's father went the night I told him I was pregnant.'

'Do you . . . have you been out with anyone since?'

'You're joking, aren't you? With one here and one on the way?'

I shrugged. 'Well, what do you do with yourself, then?'

'Watch telly and keep an eye on her,' she said. 'That's all there is. What d'you think you're going to do, then?'

'I was wondering about going back to school.'

'They won't have you,' she said scornfully. 'And who d'you think'll mind your kiddie for you?'

I shook my head, not knowing. Mum wouldn't, that was for sure. She liked her job too much.

Izzy reached for Gabriel and hauled her up, shaking her by the shoulder until she snivelled. 'Have you got to go into Bed and Breakfast when you get out?' she asked me.

I shook my head. 'I'm going home to my mum's.'

'You're lucky. B and B is the pits. I was in a place for two months – disgusting, it was. Don't let them put you in B and B. You don't even get a telly.'

'Why couldn't you go home?'

'Me mum got married again, didn't she? Her new bloke wouldn't have me in the house.'

'That's not fair!' I said, shocked.

'You tell them that.'

As Gabriel disappeared out of the door, Izzy suddenly shrieked her name at the top of her voice. I realised that people were looking at us.

'I'd better get back upstairs to the baby,' I said.

'To little Gabriel?' She caught hold of her toddler. 'Hear that? You're having a new baby named after you.'

The child stared up at me. Her jumper had dried egg down the front of it and her nose had run so much that all along her top lip it was red and sore.

'Yes, well, I haven't quite decided on his name yet,' I said, vowing that my baby would *never* look like her, that my beautiful baby would never be grubby and ugly and scruffy and snotty.

'Come over and see me if you want,' she offered. 'I'm in Sidney Street. Number twelve, Colet Court – the flats at the end. It's nothing fantastic, like, but it'll be something for you to do.' She rolled her eyes, 'You wait. It's dead boring being at home with kids. Or I could come round to you if you like.'

I had a vision of her turning up with the undesirable Gabriel and another grubby baby in tow and was just about to make an excuse when I realised I was being as snobbish and horrible as my mum. I might need friends. I *did* need friends.

I nodded. 'Yeah, I'll come round sometime. And good luck with the new baby.'

'Cheers.'

'Goodbye, Gabriel,' I said as I went out, but she just grizzled and turned her face into her mum's skirt again.

I went back up to my ward in the lift, promising myself that I wasn't going to get like her and that he, my baby, wasn't going to get like Gabriel. My baby would be like the babies in advertisements: happy and shiny and fresh-looking. I'd play with him and teach him nursery rhymes and read him stories, and when he was older we'd talk about everything and I'd listen to his problems and be his best friend. When he started going out with girls I'd tell him he must treat them properly and never, ever risk getting anyone pregnant. I'd say that, although I loved him to bits, wouldn't be without him for anything and would do the best for him that I could, having a fifteen year old mum wasn't honestly and truly the greatest start in the world.

When I got back to the ward, Susie had arrived to see me and was chatting to the Sister behind the nurses' counter.

I went into the nursery, collected the baby and pushed him back beside my bed. A new girl had arrived in the bed next to mine and, thinking she looked about my age, I went to speak to her. She turned out to be twenty-two, though, and married, and quite posh. She cut me dead when I told her I was fifteen.

'Good heavens,' she said, 'didn't you have lessons about contraception at school?'

I stared at her. 'I must have been off that day,' I said.

'I should say you were,' she said in a shocked voice.

I turned my back and went to my own bed. Stupid *cow*.

Susie came in, gave me a kiss and picked up the baby. She looked him all over, cooing in admiration.

'I'm not looking at him as a social worker,' she said. 'I'm just admiring him.'

'Isn't he gorgeous?'

She nodded. 'And he's going to be brainy, too. Look at that wide forehead.' We looked, and admired, then she said, 'Talking of brains, have you got your exam results yet?'

I shook my head. 'I've lost track of when we hear. Next week, I think.'

She raised her eyebrows. 'I wonder how you've done . . . '

'Badly, I should think. My mind was on other things. My mind was in my tummy.'

'What are you calling him?'

I sighed. 'Dunno. Not Gabriel. Maybe Robbie or Stevie or Gavin.'

'And how's your mum behaving herself?'

I smiled. 'Okay. Not at all bad.'

'See – I told you, didn't I? I told you she'd come round.'

'Only just! Even when I'd had him she was still going on about having him adopted.'

'Hmm,' Susie said. 'She told me she thought that was what *you* wanted.'

We paused as two huge bouquets of flowers, one white and one pink, were delivered to the girl in the bed next to mine. Susie looked over to her and said, 'They look wonderful!' and the girl said, smugly, 'Honestly! My husband's so extravagant!'

I pretended to have found something interesting to look at in the corridor. I'd only had the basket of flowers from Luke, and a bunch out of the garden from my mum, whereas Mrs Smugface was obviously going to have a complete flower shop on her locker before the end of the day.

'Now,' Susie said to me, 'as I said, I've spoken to your mum about arrangements, and we've had a case conference about you in the office.'

'What for? What's that mean?' I said in alarm. I dreaded finding that the baby was going to be taken away from me, or that limits were going to be put on the amount of time I could have him for. It still seemed incredible that they'd let me have this baby all to myself. To keep for ever.

'It doesn't mean anything bad,' Susie said. 'It's just routine. We – the Social Services – need to know that the baby is going to be looked after properly and brought up in a safe environment.'

'Oh, he will be,' I said, nodding vigorously.

'I know that. I know your mum will keep an eye on you both.'

I pulled a face. 'Too much of an eye, I expect.'

'That's better than getting no help at all. I mean, if you told me that you were going to live with that baby in a squat or a Hell's Angels chapter house then we might have to put a care order on you both. As it is, though, you'll be living in a secure home with your own mum and, once you're sixteen, legally able to look after the baby yourself. I won't be needed as your social worker any longer.'

I grinned. 'Once you've gone I might run wild.'

'You might. But you might not have the money,' Susie said. 'Have you given any thought to how hard up you're going to be?'

I shrugged. 'I'll get a job in the evenings or something. Mum will mind the baby.'

Susie raised her eyebrows. 'You'd better check that out with her first. Have you heard from Luke?'

I nodded. 'He asked me to marry him.'

Susie laughed. 'You turned him down, I hope.'

'Well, I haven't yet,' I said. 'I'm going to write to him.'

'You must try and stay friends with him,' Susie said. 'Apart from anything else, your son will need a father. And besides, Luke's parents may want to settle some money on the baby. You'll honestly need all the help you can get. You'll get a pittance from the Government.'

As she spoke, one of the porters from downstairs appeared holding a little wooden crate.

'Mrs Carteret?' he asked.

From behind me, from Mrs Smugface, I heard, 'That's me!'

The porter handed over the crate thing to her and

she said in a loud voice, 'Oh, champagne and choco-
lates. How gorgeous!'

I pulled a face at Susie. I didn't care. I had my baby.
I didn't need anything else.

CHAPTER FIVE

Ward 7 (but only just)
St Brides' General Hospital

August 18th

Dear Dad,

I'm packed and ready to go home from hospital.

I've been waiting all morning for a doctor to come and give me the okay, so I could ring mum to get her to collect me, but now I've heard that he'll be another hour getting up here because of some emergency or other. I've already given the baby 'one last bottle' twice.

Your grandson is perfect and sleeps nearly all the time. I had a lovely letter from Auntie Lorna and she sent me some money. On the way home Mum's taking me into Mothercare to spend it.

I can't wait to get home and get sorted out. My

exam results should be here this week. (Not really looking forward to those!)

I was just going to say that I still hadn't decided on a name for the baby when it suddenly hit me. I've been thinking of really modern names all the time (Zak, Dean, Dion) and Mum's been saying that trendy names are all very well but they go out of fashion. Then, just when I was writing your envelope I suddenly thought of something! The best thing would be an old-fashioned name that's got trendy . . . so you're the first to be told that I'm going to call the baby after you: JACK!

Lots of love, Megan and Jack

'Well,' Mum said, pursing her lips. 'I can't say he deserves to have a baby named after him. Not seeing as he left us for someone else ten years ago.'

'I'm not exactly naming the baby after him,' I said. I shifted the baby – Jack – from one shoulder to the other. 'I just think it's a nice name. Don't you?'

'It's all right,' she said sniffily.

'Well, I couldn't name him after you, could I?' I said. 'I could hardly call him Christine.'

'Don't be silly,' she said. She shrugged. 'Well, it's entirely your decision.'

'Jack it is, then,' I said.

We were in Mothercare. I hadn't quite managed to tell her the baby's name on the taxi ride from the hospital, but here in the shop there were other things going on to distract her.

She suddenly looked down at the clothes I was clutching in my free hand.

'What on earth are those things?'

'Dungarees. Little tiny denim dungarees. Aren't they gorgeous ?'

'But he won't be wanting them for another couple of years.'

'Yes, he will. He'll be crawling soon.'

We each looked at what the other was carrying. Mum had a wire basket containing vests, towelling nappies and boring long nightie things – and I was holding a purple T-shirt, a tiny baseball cap and the dungarees.

'Those things you've got there aren't practical,' she said. 'You want things you can put in and out of the washing machine. And for goodness sake use a basket. You're going to drop that baby. His head's going all over the place. Didn't they tell you in hospital that you have to support a baby's head?'

As if he'd heard her, Jack gave a whimper and woke up with a start, his arms jerking outwards.

'See! He feels insecure like that. Let me have him here,' she said, trying to take him.

'No!' I spoke more loudly than I meant to, because I'd only been out of the hospital for an hour and already she was getting on my nerves.

Hearing me shout, Jack began to cry.

'There!' Mum said. 'I told you.'

I joggled him a bit to calm him down. He cried louder and in my confusion I dropped the clothes I was carrying. I wasn't used to him screaming; he'd always been so good in hospital.

Mum made a grab for him. 'Careful! Careful!' she said, as people began to look round at us. 'That's a baby you've got there, not a stuffed toy.'

I glared at her. 'I know!'

She bent down to pick up the dropped clothes. 'People are staring at you,' she said in a cross whisper. 'You're making an exhibition of yourself.'

'No. They're staring at *you*,' I said. 'Anyway, I don't care if they are.'

She turned away and I put my little finger in Jack's mouth to give him something to suck on.

'Are your hands clean?' Mum demanded.

'Yes, they are!' I walked away from her to the other end of the shop, rocking Jack in my arms and trying to get him to stop crying.

'It's the change of routine,' a woman said kindly, pausing beside me with what looked like two grand-children in tow. 'They're always the same when you go out shopping. They don't like change, you see.'

I nodded. Everyone knew things about babies except me.

'Get him a dummy,' she said, walking away. 'That's what he needs.'

Jack had set up a proper roar now. As I lurked by the changing rooms, suddenly feeling tired and fed up, I could see Mum at the front of the shop, talking to one of the shop assistants. My legs were aching and I had a horrible dragging feeling in my stomach, as if there was a weight in there pulling my insides downwards.

I caught sight of myself in one of the mirrors and almost screamed with horror. I looked a total and utter *mess*. Mum had brought up two lots of clothes to the hospital the day before: jeans, a short skirt, and a skimpy T-shirt. I hadn't been able to get into the jeans or skirt, and the T-shirt had looked utterly gross with my bulging bosoms, so she'd taken them back and brought in the only skirt I had that was bigger, which happened to be my old school skirt. I was wearing this now, with the zip right open so my still-huge tummy could fit in it, with a long white sweatshirt over the top. I reckoned Ellie had been wearing the sweatshirt while I'd been away at Lorna's, though, because it was more grey than white and had gone all wavy around the bottom.

To add to this general gorgeousness, my hair consisted of two dark, greasy rats' tails hanging down either side of my head, my face looked all puffed up, and I had three big red spots on my chin. I looked utterly foul.

I sighed and sank down onto a chair in the changing rooms. My arm was aching as well. Even though Jack was only light, holding him in one position was killing me. I shifted him over onto my other arm. Why was he crying? I'd thought he'd love being taken round the shops.

Mum appeared in the doorway of the changing rooms. 'Look, love,' she said, 'I've put all the stuff we've chosen by the till and the girl is wrapping it up now.' She spoke to me soothingly. 'Shall I take Jack so you can go and look at the prams?'

'I 'spose so,' I said. I stood up and handed him over, secretly glad to do so.

'You go and choose the one you want. I've got the girl to call us a taxi and it'll be here in ten minutes.'

'Okay,' I said wearily.

I went to the place where the prams, push-chairs and buggies were and wheeled a few up and down. I couldn't see much difference in them. Besides, I was past caring. As long as they went along and you could put a baby in them, they'd be all right. I looked at the price tags, picked the cheapest and wheeled it to the cash desk.

'I hope you haven't got the cheapest,' Mum said, raising her voice above Jack's crying. 'It's a false economy, you know.' She looked the one I'd chosen up and down, and tugged at the stripy material. 'You want one that will last.'

Exasperated, I shoved it at her. 'You go and choose, then!' I said. 'You seem to know everything about everything. Why don't you pick what *you* want!'

It was evening and Jack was still crying. He'd stopped while I'd fed him, but after dropping off to sleep for a few moments, he'd started up again. Dimly, I wondered what it would be like if it went on all night. And night after night.

Since we'd been home, Mum had been hovering over me like a bird of prey, watching everything I did. Was the bottle too warm/too cold? Had it been mixed properly? Did he have something sticking in him? Did he have wind? Hadn't they told me about gripe water in the hospital? Why didn't I put warmer bootees on him?

I felt I was going to start screaming myself, soon. To add to all this, Ellie was hanging over the cot with worried eyes saying her friend's mum's baby never cried like this; was he ill? What was *wrong* with him?

We picked him up and put him down by turn. We tried him in the carry-cot, on the bed, on the settee, on the carpet.

'Let's give him a nice warm bath,' Mum said finally. 'Maybe that will soothe him.'

'I think we ought to call the doctor,' I said. I'd started biting my nails that afternoon. I'd never done it before.

'Don't be ridiculous!' Mum said, pulling my fingers out of my mouth. 'You can't call a doctor out just because a baby cries a bit.'

'What is it, then?'

'I think he feels insecure,' Mum said. 'He's been shoved from pillar to post today and – I know you don't like me saying it – but you hold him so awkwardly, as if he's a loaf of bread under your arm. A baby needs to feel safe.'

'Shall I pick him up again?' Ellie asked.

'Oh, not yet!' I said.

The phone rang and as no one else jumped to answer it, I went out to the hall. Just as I picked it up, someone knocked at the front door.

'Hello? Hang on, please,' I said to whoever it was on the phone, and opened the door.

Mrs Brewster – Ellie and I called her Witches Brew – from the flat underneath us stood there holding a letter.

'This arrived this morning,' she said. 'Whoever it's from has put the wrong number on it.'

I took it and recognised Luke's writing on the envelope.

'Thanks very much,' I said.

'I can hear a baby crying . . . ' Witches Brew said, looking at me enquiringly.

I didn't reply, and she tried to look past me and down the hall. I knew Mum had told one of the neighbours that I'd gone away because I'd got asthma. I wondered if it was her and decided I didn't care if it was.

'Yes, it is a baby crying,' I said.

She nodded, pleased. 'A new baby, it sounds like. Have you got visitors?'

'No. He's mine,' I said.

Her eyes widened.

'He's a new baby and he's gorgeous and he's mine,' I said defiantly. 'Goodbye.'

I closed the door on her. Mum called, 'Who's that?' but I ignored her.

'Hello?' I said into the telephone.

There was some giggling at the other end. 'It's me,' Claire said. 'Have you got your results?'

'What?' It took me a moment or two to think what she was talking about. I was just so full up with baby.

'GCSEs!'

'Oh. No,' I said. 'I thought it was tomorrow.'

'We all went up the school today. They were giving out the results there.'

'Oh,' I said again. Thanks for asking me, I thought. 'How did you get on, then?'

'Josie didn't get *any!*' Claire said, and there was a scuffle and I heard her say, 'Shut up a minute.' She added, 'Josie says to tell you that she knew she wasn't getting any because she just dossed about, and she doesn't care.'

'What did you get?'

'Two Bs, four Cs and two Es,' Claire said.

'That's good.'

'Is that your baby crying?'

'Yeah. His name's Jack, by the way.'

'Aaaah,' Claire said. 'Blimey, isn't he making a racket?'

'He's just waiting to be fed,' I lied. 'I'd better go.'

'Just a sec,' Claire said. 'Have you heard about Luke?'

'What?' I said sharply. 'What about him?'

'He's up in Sheffield.'

I was stunned into silence. I looked at the letter in my hand. It had a Sheffield postmark.

'You still there?' Claire asked. 'Apparently his mum and dad decided to buy him a flat up there instead of renting one, and he's gone with them to sort it out.'

'Oh. Right,' I said.

'So you won't be . . . ' She lowered her voice. 'Look, I do like Luke but I'd never have tried anything on with him. Not if you were going out with him.'

'That's okay,' I said. 'I knew it wasn't really on. I mean, I just think he went a bit daft when he saw the baby. I knew his mum and dad wouldn't let him get a flat with me.'

There was another silence. 'Still, you've got the baby!' she said cheerfully.

'Yeah. Course.'

'I'd better go. We're going down the Square to see who's down there and find out what results they've got.'

'Have a good time,' I said automatically. And thanks *very* much for not collecting my results, I thought . . .

CHAPTER SIX

17 Maybury Court
Castleton

August 20th

Dear Luke,

First of all, I'd better tell you that I'm calling the baby Jack. I hope you like it. It's my dad's name.

Thanks for your letter and for giving me your address in Sheffield. I knew you were up there before I got your letter, because Claire rang to tell me. (By the way, you do know she fancies you, don't you? I don't suppose it matters if I tell you now.)

When you didn't come back to visit me in hospital or contact me again, I knew that you weren't up for it, that we weren't *really* going to set up home together. To be honest, my mum hit the roof when she thought we were getting married, she said it was the stupidest thing she'd ever heard. She *said* your mum and dad wouldn't allow it, and it looks as if she was spot on if they've packed you off to Sheffield early. And they're buying you a flat up there, too! They must be dead worried that I might get my claws into you.

It's okay, though. I mean, I could be a real cow and go mad at you for letting me down, but almost as soon as you left the ward I realised that it would never work. I know you asked me on the spur of the moment, without really thinking about it. I bet you panicked when you got home (especially after all your mates telling you that you had a screw loose). I know you're not really ready to have a wife – and I don't think I'm ready to have a husband, either. (Or a baby, for that matter, but that's different.)

My mum said that practically all teenage marriages end in divorce. So there's really no point, is there? We'd start off trying to do the right thing by the baby, but end up being unhappy and hating each other, and in the end splitting up and making the baby miserable anyway.

Having said all this, I do want to stay friends. We *must* stay friends, because of Jack. My social worker says it's really important that we do, so that he knows who you are and who his family is. She said it might be a nice idea for me to take Jack round to see your mum and dad! (Don't worry, I wouldn't dare.)

I've only been back home a couple of days and everything is a mess; I don't know what way up I am. Jack isn't in a routine yet, and being out of the hospital seems to have muddled him. He's much hungier, and more unsettled, and keeps crying all the time. He was up at two o'clock this morning for a feed and now it's about six-thirty and he's just had another bottle. I feel bloody knackered but just can't sleep, so am writing to you instead.

Anyway, hope you get on okay up there, and me and Jack will see you when you come home at Christmas.

Love from Megan

I put Luke's letter on the side, ready to post, and looked round the kitchen. It was a mess, full of half-empty baby bottles, bits of sterilising equipment, soggy bibs and baby clothes. Packets of disposable baby-wipes and liners were piled along the dresser and there was a faint smell of pooey nappies in the air.

I still hadn't found time to wash my hair and I felt

sticky and horrible. I couldn't understand why Jack was being such a pain since we'd come out of hospital; why he kept crying all the time.

When I'd got up about five o'clock I found I'd run out of bottles of milk, so I'd blearily mixed one up with dried milk formula. I couldn't have done it properly, though, because lumps clogged up the teat, making Jack yell in frustration because he couldn't get at the milk.

When, at last, he'd finished feeding, I'd changed his nappy, cleaned him up a bit and because it was practically morning, decided to get him dressed. I'd put on his new dungarees (even though they were far too big) and he'd immediately been sick down them, so I'd had to change his clothes again right down to his vest. He'd then fallen asleep in his carrycot and I'd tried to sleep but been unable to.

At eight-thirty, Ellie put her head round the door.

'How long have you been up?' she said.

'Dunno.' I yawned. 'I've lost all sense of time. I don't even know what day it is.'

She produced a camera. 'I want to take some photos of you both. We've got to send some to dad.'

I let out a scream. 'Not with me looking like this, you don't!' Apart from everything else, I was wearing a dressing gown with baby sick down it. 'At least wait until I'm washed and dressed.'

Ellie hung over the cot. 'Shall I watch him while you go and have a bath and wash your hair, then?'

I nodded.

'Can I take him for a walk?'

'Not yet,' I said. 'We'll go out later on. When I'm ready.'

Mum came in and peered into the carry-cot. 'He's not too hot, is he, Megan? He looks a bit flushed.'

Without waiting for a reply (not that I had one) she went straight to the window.

'I thought the school would have sent them out first class.'

'What?' I looked up at her blankly.

'The results!'

'Oh, yes,' I said without enthusiasm. I'd forgotten all about them. Exam results weren't the big thing in my life any more. It was funny: just a few months ago I'd been living and breathing GCSEs: exams, course work and reading lists. Since last April, though, when I'd first found out I was pregnant, they hardly seemed to matter at all.

'I think the postman comes about now.' She gave a little cry. 'Oh no, he's right down the end of the road.

73

He's gone by!'

I tucked a greasy lock of hair behind my ear, trying to look as if I cared one way or the other.

'Oh, no!' Mum said again. 'Another day to wait.'

'Maybe they'll come second post,' I said, yawning again. 'Thing is, Mum, they don't really matter much now, do they?'

'Of course they matter!'

'Why do they? I'm not going to be able to go into the Sixth and start doing A Levels next month, am I? Not unless I can find a baby-minder.'

'I'll mind him,' Ellie said.

We ignored her.

'These exams are *very* important,' Mum said. 'They can give us an indication of your future.'

I shrugged. 'Okay,' I said. 'But I'm going to have a long bath and wash my hair. I'll *die* if I don't wash my hair,' I added.

'You'd better make the most of it,' Mum said, 'because when I'm back at work and Ellie's at school you'll be here on your own. You won't be able to leave that baby and go off and have long baths then.'

'What, will I be tied to the cot? Not allowed to even *move?*'

'You wait,' Mum said, 'it'll feel like that sometimes.' She picked up the envelope from the dresser. 'You've written to Luke, then? You've told him you're not marrying him, have you?'

I nodded. I couldn't be bothered to say that it was him who'd told me, actually.

Mum tutted. 'Two scraps of kids. As if he would have been the slightest bit of good to you.'

I nodded because it was what she expected and, yawning hugely, went into the bathroom.

The bath was bliss. I used masses of bubble bath, washed my hair and then just lay back and played mermaids, letting my hair float across the water.

Along the hallway, I heard Jack wake up and begin to cry. I slipped a little further under the foam so that my ears were below the waterline and I couldn't hear.

I closed my eyes. My body was my own and I was me again.

Everything was unreal, it had all been a dream.

I moved my legs so that the water lapped across my body in a soothing, rhythmic way. I was me again and I was getting ready for a night out. Claire and I were going to meet some of the girls, and we were going to the cinema, to see something funny. Behind us in the cinema would be a group of boys and they'd start chatting to us and one of them – the best-looking one

– would keep staring at me. When the film finished he'd ask for my phone number and say that he's going to ring me soon.

The baby had all been a dream.

I'd be going on to the Sixth to do A Levels, and next year Claire and I would go Inter-Railing, and do twelve countries in three weeks. We'd meet boys all along the way, boys from England and foreign boys, and have a real laugh. We'd be broke when we got back, but we'd be really brown, and have had hundreds of adventures and be able to speak French really well.

It had all been a dream.

I'd be going to Glastonbury next June and I'd stay up for three nights in a row and hear some fantastic bands and have weird food and meet this gorgeous bloke who was a roadie and who'd give me back-stage passes. While I was there I'd be photographed rolling in the mud and the photos would be spotted by a model agency who'd sign me up, and then I'd be going all over the world on exciting assignments. I'd still take my A Levels, though, because I wanted to go to university, which would be like Glastonbury all the time.

It had all been a dream.

The bathroom door opened and Ellie came in and said something. Slowly, reluctantly, I slid upwards so that I could hear her.

'Jack's screaming his head off,' she announced. 'Mum says she's going to give him another bottle but she wants you to scrub the teats out properly with a bottle brush first.'

I stared at her blearily through the steam.

'She says you've got to come *now*.'

I sighed. My wobbly, bloated boobs stuck out above the water and I could see the livid scar on my tummy where Jack had been cut out.

It hadn't been a dream. I *had* had a baby and I had to leave my dreams and go and look after him.

CHAPTER SEVEN

17 Maybury Court
Castleton

August 25th

Dear Amy,

How long did it take you to get into a routine? I'm asking because I've been home nearly a week and I'm still in a big muddle. My mum's gone back to work now and the Health Visitor has been coming in, and every morning I try and *try* to be sorted out and organised ready for her, but I never am. Whatever time she arrives I'm a mess of nappies, bottles, baby clothes and screaming baby.

I'm nearly always in my dressing gown because I can never find anything to wear. I spend hours pulling clothes on and off, but have only found about two things that fit me. Everything else has to be safety-pinned together and the things that *do* fit only last about half an hour and then Jack is sick down them.

When I was in hospital I remember thinking that it would be a doddle – being a mum, I mean. They're always saying it's hard work, but I thought they must be telling you that just to put you off. Lying about playing with a baby all day – how could that be hard work?

Bloody hell, though! I know now. I mean, I do love Jack very much (I did tell you I was calling him Jack, didn't I?) but I find it so difficult coping with every-thing. He was so good when we were in hospital and I thought he would just stay like that. But practically the minute we got out of the hospital gates, he start-ed. I've had to buy him a dummy. Mum hates it and keeps hiding it, but I don't care as long as it keeps him quiet.

What grades did you get in your exams? I still haven't got my results. After a lot of fussing around (and waiting for them to come from my school) Mum discovered that they'd been sent from the educational unit to my Auntie Lorna's house. She's now gone off to Italy, so Mum then had to ring the Education people and ask then to send down a copy. It's on its way now, apparently, and I'm all prepared for another scene when it arrives.

What have your friends been like? Have they been round to see you since you got out of hospital? My best friend, Claire, came into the hospital and has rung me a couple of times, but that's all. When she came to visit, this other friend, Josie, came with her and all they spoke about was what they were doing and what a good time they were having (without me). Claire and I have been best friends for years, but this Josie has been trying to edge in between us for a long time, and now she's got a golden opportunity.

I suppose it's different for you, because you've still got your boyfriend around (by the way, in the end Luke didn't stay and get us a flat, he went up to Sheffield instead!). Does your boyfriend take Meredith out, and does he change his nappies? Do you do nice things like take the baby out for walks together?

I hope Luke isn't going to be my only boyfriend ever. My mum reckons no boy will want to take on someone else's baby. What do you think?

One day I'd like another try at sex, too. I remember the night I fell for Jack and it wasn't anything to write home about. Bit of a dead loss, in fact. I hope it's better next time. I tell you what, though, I'll be a sight more careful if there is a next time. I won't do it

81

unless (a) I'm really sure I love him, (b) I know the relationship is going to last and (c) one of us is using something. No, on second thoughts, BOTH of us is using something.

Lorna sent me a cheque to buy a pram and carry-cot and other stuff. She wrote to me saying that she was so pleased when she found out I was keeping the baby that she drank a whole bottle of champagne to celebrate. This is because, twenty years ago, she had a baby and had it adopted. She's never got over it and told me that she thinks about her son every day. It was her who really made me think how awful giving up a baby would be. (No one else in my family knows about this!)

My mum gets on my nerves but she's much nicer to me since I had Jack, and I'm getting on better with my sister as well. I just wish I could get *sorted*. There doesn't seem to be anything in my life except BABY, just the one thing. So why can't I get organised?

I'm writing this after the four-in-the-morning feed. He still wakes around this time – does Meredith? I can never get back to sleep once it's started to get light, so I write my letters then. Write back soon.

Lots of love, Megan

I stared out of the window, nibbling at my nails. It was raining and, because I didn't have a proper rain cover on the push-chair, I couldn't go out and post my letter to Amy.

I felt pretty sorry for myself, actually. Mum was at work, Ellie had gone away with her best friend's family, and I was on my own with Jack and he'd just started crying again.

It seemed to me that babies only did four things: eat, wee, poo and cry.

The Health Visitor, and Susie, both said that he was healthy enough and not to worry, that most babies had a crying time. The Health Visitor said I ought to pick him up whenever he cried, but Susie said he could be left to yell for a while. She didn't say how long 'a while' was, though.

The dummy wasn't much help. Sometimes he cried so hard that he spat the dummy out and then it would get lost down the mattress.

I loved him hugely, of course, and however much he cried that would never change, but it was really different from how I thought it would be when I was in hospital.

He wasn't always crying. Not every minute. It just seemed like that.

Now I was at home and had time to think about things, I'd started to feel scared. At first I was just really excited at the thought of being a person with a baby, but now it sometimes seemed that there was nothing ahead of me: no Inter-Railing or university or boyfriends or clothes or *fun*. I always used to have things to look forward to, things coming up that were going to happen when I was a bit older. Now all the things I used to dream about and look forward to have disappeared.

Every penny I had went on Jack. I got a measly allowance which nearly all went on disposable nappies and there was never anything left over.

I traced my finger down the window, tracking a raindrop, thinking that even if there *was* money over, even if I suddenly got a big wodge of money to spend, I'd have to use it to buy a proper cot for Jack, or baby clothes or toys.

And if I got a bigger wodge still, what could I do with it? I couldn't go out anywhere, couldn't go on holiday, couldn't get all dressed up and go out with my mates, because Jack was there like a great big full-stop.

As Jack's crying increased, I felt tears of self-pity come into my eyes. I didn't *want* to be stuck indoors with a baby to look after and washing to do and bottles to make up and nappies to change, I wanted to be out somewhere with Claire, having a laugh.

I sighed, turned away from the window and put the TV on, trying to ignore Jack. I was getting to be a right old slouch these days; I saw more of the daytime TV presenters than I did anyone else. I felt I knew them, that they were my friends. How sad was that?

A soap that I'd seen the day before came on, and I turned the set off. I picked up one of the many baby-care books I seemed to have accumulated, and turned to what this particular book called, 'Those Precious First Months'.

As I read, trying to work out why Jack hadn't got into a 'manageable sleeping pattern', he began to really yell. I picked him out of the little seat Ellie had managed to get from a jumble sale, and held him at arm's length.

'You're a little horror,' I said to him. 'You cry and cry for no reason.'

He screamed on with his face screwed up, all red and blotched. What was wrong with him? He wasn't due for another feed for *ages*.

I sighed and laid him on my shoulder, feeling his wet nose and mouth on my neck, dampening my

T-shirt. I wondered if Izzy had had her baby yet, and what it would be like to have *two*. That was another thing, I'd always imagined that I'd have two or three children, but Jack would have to be an only child. There was no way that I was having a brother or sister for him for years and years. Or ever.

I heard the postman in the hall and, with Jack still pressed against my shoulder, went to the door.

There, on the mat, was the brown window envelope Mum had been waiting for. My results.

I wondered for an instant if I could just push it under the mat and hide it. That way Mum would have to apply all over again and it would give me a few weeks' respite.

I bent down to pick it up. Sometime or other she'd have to know. I might as well get it over with . . .

I tore open the envelope and pulled out the printed sheet. Jack's head lolled against mine, getting in the way of my view. I moved the result paper to the other hand and stared at it.

I had five As, two Bs and a C.

'Oh my God!' I shrieked. I couldn't believe it. Just couldn't believe it. I'd thought I'd maybe get a couple of Cs for my best subjects, and the rest would be Es or worse.

Jack, startled by my shout, began crying again. I scrambled around to find his dummy, shoved it in and picked up the phone to ring Mum.

'What's wrong?' she said immediately. 'Is the baby all right?'

'Nothing's wrong,' I said. 'I've got my results, that's all.'

'Oh dear,' she said. 'Okay. You'd better tell me what they are. By the time I come home from work I might have got over it.'

I put on a reluctant voice. 'Are you sure you want to hear?'

She put her hand over the phone and I heard her say to someone else in the office, 'My daughter's results have arrived.'

'Are they that bad?' she said to me.

'Pretty bad,' I said. 'Five As, two Bs and a C.'

'*What?*'

I repeated it, then I went through the subjects one by one, giving each grade by turn.

She was silent for a long time, then she started crying. Started *crying!*

'What's up?' I said, bewildered. 'Why are you crying? They're fantastic results. I thought you'd be really pleased.'

She went on crying, then I heard her put the phone down and blow her nose. When she picked it up, she said, 'I *am* pleased, that's the trouble.'

'What d'you mean?'

'These results mean that you're capable of brilliant things. You could have easily got three A Levels and gone to university. And now you won't. You've thrown it all away! Your whole life!'

And with that she started crying again.

Jack's dummy dropped onto the floor and he started again too, so I just put the phone down and went into the kitchen to start preparing a bottle for him.

There was just no pleasing some people, was there? Suppose I'd got terrible results, what would she have been like then?

And talk about over-reaction: *ruined my whole whole life*. Why did she have to be so dramatic about things?

But I knew what she meant.

CHAPTER EIGHT

I wriggled and squirmed and at last managed to get my jeans over my thighs. By taking it slowly, an inch at a time, I pulled them higher and higher until they at last reached my waist. Try as I might, though, I couldn't do them up.

Never mind. I had a long T-shirt which came right down over my bottom and would cover everything. It was only plain white cotton from the cheap-jack shop in town – mum said it wouldn't last more than one wash – but it looked fairly all right if you glanced at it quickly. It looked new, anyway, and not crumpled or faded or stretched like everything else I had.

My hair had been in mum's heated rollers while I'd been in the bath, and it looked quite good: shiny, bouncy and just a bit tousled, and I'd put on make-up for the first time in months. The finished result was okayish. Not too bad.

'He's asleep,' Mum said, coming into my bedroom without knocking. 'He's in the carry-cot and out for the count.'

'I should think so,' I said. 'He's been awake all afternoon. Hasn't closed his eyes since this morning.'

'He's still got that rash all down his cheeks, hasn't he? When you take him to the Clinic tomorrow I should mention it.' She looked me up and down. 'You look very nice, love. That loose fringe you've got shows up your eyes. You've got lovely dark eyes.' She pursed her lips a bit, 'Like your dad's.'

I grinned to myself.

'What time are they coming?'

'Seven-thirty.'

She looked at her watch. 'Have you written to your dad?' she asked.

'Not yet.'

'You've got time now, then.'

I groaned.

'Do it now and I can post it tomorrow from work. Just a few lines. Don't you want to give him your good news?'

'Yeah, but . . . '

'Just sit down and do it,' she said firmly. 'It'll take you two minutes.'

She disappeared and I got out my pad.

August 28th

Dear Dad,

Just a short note to let you know how I got on with my exams. I got five As, two Bs and a C! I couldn't believe it (nor could Mum).

I can't write much at the moment because I'm getting ready to go out. When I rang my friend Claire to tell her my results, she said there was a crowd of them going out to celebrate theirs, and I could go with them if I liked.

Nearly everyone else got their results a couple of weeks ago, but as some were away they've only just got round to organising anything. It will be brilliant to be out! I don't feel I've been anywhere for *years*.

I know it's going to be a bit funny facing everyone, but I've got to do it sometime and maybe it'll be better to see them all at once.

Jack is changing and growing all the time. He's lovely, even though he drives me mad sometimes. He cries a lot still, but at the Clinic they told me that it might be because he's teething. Mum's just brought him in here (my bedroom) fast asleep in his carry-cot. I wish you could see him, but I still haven't got a photo because the ones that Ellie took were all out of focus. You could hardly see which one was me and which was him.

I hope all your family are well and I hope you're pleased with my results.

Lots of love, Megan and Jack

As I put the letter in its envelope, there was a ring at the doorbell.

'I'll go!' Ellie called.

I checked on Jack, wanting to make sure he was looking his best. Mum had changed the sheets on the carry-cot, and put the best blue patchwork quilt on it, and Jack looked beautiful, like a little sleeping cherub. His perfectly-shaped mouth was moving slightly, as if he was dreaming he was having a bottle, and his hair, just washed, had gone into little curly tendrils around his face.

I stared down at him, wishing he could always look like this: quiet and content and perfect.

'Here's Claire!' Ellie said from the doorway. 'And

Josie and the others . . .'

Claire stood there, beaming. 'Everyone wanted to see the baby,' she said, as seven girls crowded into my bedroom. 'You don't mind, do you?'

'Course not,' I said as they all gathered round the cot, oohing and aahing and giving little screams of surprise and amazement.

They wanted to know what giving birth to him had been like and I exaggerated it into a big drama which ended with me having the emergency Caesarean. As they listened, open-mouthed, I felt very worldly and important. I'd done something, experienced things that none of them had the least idea about.

Naomi looked round at the piled up clothes and changing table and bath and bouncy chair. 'How do you manage in here?' she said. 'This room's *tiny*.'

'It'll be worse soon,' I said. 'Somehow I've got to fit a full-size cot in.'

'Can't you move to a bigger place?' she asked.

I was just going to say that I didn't think so, when Josie, who was standing by the carry-cot, said loudly, 'I think this baby's got measles!'

'It's not measles,' I said quickly, 'just a rash.'

'You want to watch out,' she said. 'My cousin had a baby when she was fourteen and she didn't look after him properly so they took him away. They put him with foster parents.'

Everyone gawped and I felt myself going red. 'It's not because I'm not looking after him properly,' I said. 'That's a horrible thing to say. It's a heat rash. You can't help them getting things like that.'

There was a short silence.

'D'you think we'd better go?' Claire said. 'We want to make sure we get in.'

I was just getting my jacket out of the wardrobe when I noticed Josie whispering something to Naomi. They both started giggling.

I thought it was something about Jack, and I felt myself going red again. I wished Josie hadn't come. I'd never much liked her and since I'd had Jack I didn't like her at all.

'What's up with you two?' Claire asked them. 'Stop messing about.'

Josie whispered something in Claire's ear. Claire looked embarrassed.

'What's the matter?' I said, half-defiantly. If Josie said anything else horrible I was going to tell her to piss off, I really was.

'It's . . . well, you're . . .' Claire pointed to her own bust, and then mine. 'I think you're leaking or something,' she said awkwardly.

Josie snorted with laughter, the others just gave embarrassed half-smiles.

Scarlet, I looked down at myself, then pulled open my cupboard, got out a bra and an old T-shirt and ran into the bathroom.

I ripped off my clothes, feeling hot and bothered. I thought I'd finished with all the leaking business, so I'd stopped putting a shield in my bra. And to come through when they were there . . . Oh *God*.

I washed, changed, and sat on the edge of the bath, feeling sick and miserable. I didn't want to go out now. It was going to be awful. I didn't fit in, I didn't even like them any more.

There was a tap on the door. 'You all right, Megan?' Claire said. 'Look, don't worry about that . . . what happened. Don't take any notice of Josie. She's just being stupid.'

I didn't reply. I was wondering how much of this Mum and Ellie could hear.

'Come on! No one will say anything else about it, Megan! We're going to have a good time. Come on, you deserve a night out. You said you were looking forward to it.'

I hesitated. I *did* want to go out really. I slowly got

up and opened the door.

We went to *Cascades*, this big complex in town. As well as having two night clubs, there were five cinemas and a casino and all sorts of different eating places under the same roof. On Thursdays it was under eighteens night in one of the clubs, and though it only went on until 10.30, it was still pretty good.

As we were going through the entrance hall, I saw a boy. Well, there were lots of boys milling around, but one boy in particular caught my eye. He was about eighteen, and really nice-looking, with long dark hair, smiley eyes and a very straight nose. He was with some other boys going into the bar and he was laughing, and then he saw me and stopped.

'Hi!' he said, just as if he knew me.

'Hi!' I said back. I was feeling awkward, actually, because the others had been to *Cascades* loads of times and so knew the form, but I'd only been once. 'Do I know you?' I asked, because he looked vaguely familiar.

'Don't think so,' he said. He grinned. 'Are you lost? You look a bit bewildered.'

I shook my head. 'No,' I said, 'I'm fine. My mates are somewhere around.' I had my arms folded across my chest and I unfolded them and stood up straight and tried to smile normally and not be self-conscious. No one knew, I told myself. No one knew just by looking at me that I'd had a baby.

'That's okay then,' he said.

Claire, who'd gone into one of the loos, came out, saw me and came over.

'You're a fast worker,' she said to me, grinning. 'Can't leave you alone for a minute.' She linked her arm through mine to drag me off.

'See you,' I said to the boy.

'See you,' he echoed.

'Who was *he*?' Claire demanded as soon as we were out of earshot. 'How did you get chatting?'

I shrugged. I felt better. Just those two or three words with an unknown boy had given me some of my old confidence back. He'd been really nice, too. I hoped I was going to see him again.

CHAPTER NINE

17 Maybury Court
Castleton

September 3rd

Dear Lorna,

I got your postcard yesterday. It was great to hear from you and get your address. I'm up with the lark again (before the blasted lark) so I'm writing back straight away with my news.

Jack is fine, that's the first thing. And yes, I've named him after Dad and he seems to suit it. What I want to tell you is that I met a boy last week and at the moment I can't think of much else. It was my first trip out since having Jack, and it was a bit awkward at the beginning with my friends and everything, so I was almost wishing I hadn't gone. Then I saw this boy and it cheered everything up and in the end I had a good time. I saw him again when we were coming out and he bought me a coke and he was just really nice.

His name is Mark, and I don't know much about him, except he works as a reporter on the local paper and he's twenty. Do you think that's too old for me? I know he won't really be interested, because of Jack. But this doesn't mean I couldn't just go out with him a couple of times, does it? He doesn't have to know about Jack. Or should I tell him?

Of course, I might never see him again. But I think I will. I've just got that sort of feeling about him – when I saw him I felt as if I knew him. Do you know what I mean?

I'll write again immediately if anything happens. If I do see him again I want to give him my phone number. And I know what you're thinking – that I mustn't get carried away. Don't worry, although I might fancy him like mad, I'd never do anything daft. Not again.

That work you're doing on the mountain plants sounds interesting, and different from your usual stuff. I don't know what I'm ever going to do – for work, I mean. The only job I'll be able to get when Jack's old enough for nursery will be in McDonalds. Everywhere else wants A Levels. Mum is very pissed off about this, especially as (I almost forgot) I got really good results in my GCSEs: five As, two Bs and a C. I didn't expect to do this well. I reckon it was your influence!

What I wanted to ask you was, when you went out with boys (after you'd had the baby, I mean) did you tell them about it? If you did, what did they say? This girl Izzy I know said that when she tells boys, they either think they're onto a winner and try it on, or they just disappear. By the way, I hope you don't mind me talking about your baby. I'm never sure if you like me to bring it up or not. I don't want to upset you.

At first Mum said that I'd never find anyone who'd want to be with me and take Jack, but when I asked her again (I've been worried about this) she said that I *might*, but it would have to be an exceptional person. Whatever that is.

I can't stop thinking about Mark! Before Jack wakes up again and before I start on the washing I'm going to think of nothing but him for ten minutes. I'm going to *wallow*.

Write and let me know what you think about everything.

Lots of love, Megan

I found an envelope for Lorna's letter, and by that time Jack was awake and making little noises which said he was bored, fed up, and wanted something to do. You and me both, I thought. I played with him a bit, then got him up and dressed ready to go out to the post office. I'd leave the washing until later.

Jack was whingeing again by the time I'd put his outdoor clothes on, so I gave him a drop of orange juice in a bottle, found him a teddy, and tucked him into the push-chair. While I was getting changed into one of the two things I could get into, he sicked up the orange all down himself and over the push-chair apron. I changed him again, cleaned the push-chair and put him back, then had to get myself ready – all the time swishing the push-chair up and down the hall to stop him from grizzling whilst singing him a soppy nursery rhyme under my breath. It took me the best part of the morning to get out, and then, when I did get out, who should be just coming along the hall-way but old Witches Brew.

She *darted* towards me – I shouldn't think she'd ever moved so fast. 'I wondered what was going on,' she said, nodding at the push-chair. 'I said to Mrs Ford that I thought you were . . . you know . . . in the family way.'

She put her face inches from Jack's. 'Who's a lovely baby, then? Is it a girl?'

'A boy,' I said, a bit shirtily, because Jack was wearing his blue denim jacket and to my mind looked very boyish indeed. 'His name's Jack.'

Witches Brew stroked Jack's cheek. Jack stared up at her, and then suddenly beamed.

'And *what* a lovely smile!' she straightened up and eyed me. 'And will you be moving now? Getting married?'

'Not just yet,' I said. I wanted to say something sarky – like I thought I'd wait until he had a little sister before I got married – but she was bending down again and making noises at Jack and he seemed to be making them right back to her. I suddenly thought to myself that Jack didn't have a proper granny, that mum was never going to be a granny who blew bubbles and made noises.

She fingered the denim jacket disapprovingly. 'I'll knit him a cardigan,' she said. 'Pure wool. Nice and soft – not like this hard thing. You can never have too many cardigans.'

'Thanks,' I said faintly.

When I came back from the post office, Susie's green

Mini was parked outside the flats.

I liked seeing her – I liked seeing *anyone* during the day – but I always felt a bit funny about Susie. I was scared that I was on probation or something, that she was checking to see that I was looking after Jack properly.

'This isn't an official call,' she said straight away. 'I just thought I'd look in on you.'

'Do I get official calls now?'

She shook her head. 'You're pretty much on your own from now on. Sorted.'

She helped me collapse Jack's push-chair and we went up to the flat.

'You're looking a bit brighter,' she said.

I nodded. 'I'm feeling it,' I said. 'Guess why?'

'Jack's sleeping through the night?' she guessed.

'No,' I said. 'I've met someone!'

'*What?*' she looked at me, horrified.

'Oh, it's not like that,' I said. 'I've hardly spoken to him, let alone anything else.'

'I hope *not* anything else,' she said with mock sternness. 'And while we're on that subject, if things do develop you won't take any chances, will you?'

I felt myself going red. 'Of course not.'

She pointed to Jack. 'There's not really any "of

course" about it, is there?'

'No, but I wouldn't dream . . . ' I gave Jack to her while I put the kettle on. 'Anyway, it isn't like that. I've only spoken a few words to him and besides, he's not going to be interested in me.'

She smiled. 'You're a very pretty girl, Megan. He might well be interested in you.'

'But he's not going to be when he finds out about Jack, is he? Also he's twenty.' I paused, 'Is that too old? What d'you think?'

'I think,' she said slowly, 'that you haven't got quite enough going on in your life.'

'You're kidding!' I said. 'I've got loads going on. I never have a minute to myself.'

'But it's not exactly gripping, is it? Looking after a baby is a samey, boring routine. Your hands are occupied but your head is racing all over the place. You must take care that you don't go completely mad on the first boy you see.'

I handed her a mug of tea.

'You'd be far better off getting a crush on a pop star or someone. You can't get pregnant by a pop star.'

I looked at her, affronted and hurt. How could she of all people say this to me? 'You're talking about sex again,' I said, a bit humpily. 'Just because I made one mistake it doesn't mean I sleep around, you know. I've only done it twice in my life, and I'm in no hurry to do it again.'

'I'm glad to hear it,' she said. 'And I'm sorry if you thought I was . . . ' she looked at me ruefully. 'You'd be surprised how many single girls go on to have a second baby. By a different father, lots of them.'

'I know,' I said, thinking of Izzy. 'But I won't. Anyway, I can't fancy a pop star just like that. You don't get crushes on people to order. They just happen.'

'Do they?' she said. 'I'm blowed if I can remember.'

We went through into the sitting room and she put Jack – who was being good, for once – in the corner of the sofa and propped him up with cushions. He sat playing with his hands, content.

'Your mum told me about your results. Have you thought about what you're going to do next?' Susie asked.

I shook my head. I was off thinking about Mark again and I didn't want to stop and think about anything else.

'Your mother is very keen for you to do A Levels.'

'I know,' I said, 'but I can't see the point. I mean, I can't ever go to university, can I?'

'Some universities have crèches. They'll mind your

106

baby while you study.'

I shrugged. 'Yeah, but I've got to get there . . . '

'Would it be possible for you to go and live with your Auntie Lorna again? You could go to the same educational centre and take your exams while they look after Jack.'

'Blimey,' I said, surprised. 'I dunno.' I didn't know if I wanted to go away, or even if Lorna would have me. Besides . . .

'You're not thinking about this boy you've just met, are you?' Susie asked, straight away. 'Not thinking that you don't want to move because of him?'

'No,' I lied. 'No, it's not that. Lorna's away – she's in Italy working. And I don't know if Mum would want us to go away for two years. Or if Lorna would mind me staying that long.'

'Your mum would love you to get those exams.'

'Mmm . . . ' I said. 'But isn't there anywhere else I could go to take them? Anywhere near here?'

She shook her head. 'The nearest educational unit is forty miles away.'

'Oh,' I said, but I wasn't that bothered. I didn't really feel up to studying quite yet.

'In the meantime, why don't you do something during the day? Winter's coming up and you'll be like a caged lion if you don't get out occasionally. You could go to a class: keep-fit or yoga or something.'

'Can't afford it,' I said.

'Well, what about joining a mum and baby group?'

I pulled a face. 'A group meets after the Clinic at the health centre on Mondays, and I went in there and everyone was about *thirty*. I had a cup of tea and no one talked to me.'

'Well, you'll have to talk to *them*,' Susie said.

I shook my head, thinking of Mrs Smugface on my ward, knowing they'd all be like that. 'I don't want to.'

'Didn't you meet anyone at the hospital? Any other young mums?' Susie asked. Jack fell sideways onto the cushion and began to cry and she went to pick him up.

'Only one,' I said. 'A girl who used to go to my school.'

'Try and make contact with her again,' Susie said. 'It's very important you have some lifelines – places to go to get you out of the house.'

I nodded slowly. Where did I fit in now? Not with my own friends, but not with all those young mums either.

Okay, I decided. I'd go round and see Izzy. I didn't much want to, but I would.

CHAPTER TEN

It was another few days before I got myself organised enough to go out visiting. By this time everyone had gone back to school, including Ellie, and I was feeling pretty desperate.

My life was so *boring*. The evenings were okay, once Ellie and mum got in, but the days were unbelievably long – especially when they started at five in the morning. I wanted to talk to someone. Anyone. I was fed up with Richard and Judy. I wanted to see someone real.

I thought it would be better when Jack was a bit older, because then I could play with him and take him out to interesting places. The thing was, he wasn't very good company right then, because he didn't do much – apart from the four things I've mentioned before. With a bit of sleeping thrown in occasionally.

Going out visiting was an ordeal because I had to get really organised and take bottles and nappies and babywipes and all that sort of stuff with me. It was only because I thought Izzy was sure to have a changing mat and a bottle warmer there that I didn't have to cart those with me as well.

I didn't know for definite that she'd be home, of course – for all I knew she might still be in hospital having the baby. I couldn't stay in staring at packets of dried milk for much longer, though. I was going to have to chance it.

The journey was a two-bus nightmare. To catch the second one I had to walk up a steep hill pushing Jack all the way, and then wait for ages in the sun. When it eventually came there were about six people at the bus-stop but no one helped me collapse the push-chair. They just charged on in front of me, leaving me to struggle up the steps with the push-chair, Jack, his baby-travelling holdall and my own bag. The driver was in a hurry and moaned at me for not being quick enough, and when I got on and found the fare money, he looked at Jack, and then looked me up and down in a disgusted sort of way, as much as to say that he knew what I was.

It got worse. Izzy had told me her flats were grotty, and she wasn't joking. Sidney Street is part of a great big council estate, high-rise flats and all, that they're starting to pull down and improve, but they hadn't got to her bit yet.

Colet Court was at the end of the street, and just in front of it was a recycling centre with a line of bottle banks and a big skip for newspapers and cardboard. Surrounding each of these bottle banks was a sea of broken glass, and there were old newspapers blowing around and soggy bits of cardboard underfoot. Looking up at the flats, I saw that some of them had broken windows, and many had bits of sheet or towels up instead of curtains.

My heart sank. The flats where I lived weren't all that great, but at least they were private and nowhere near as bad as these. *These* flats, or ones like them, were where I'd have to live if I got a place of my own.

Seeing all this grimness, I nearly turned back, but it had been such a nightmare getting there that I thought I might as well go on. I collapsed the push-chair and, not daring to leave it downstairs, dragged it up the smelly concrete stairs to number twelve.

I tapped on the door and after a moment Izzy peered through the glass at me and then opened it.

'You're a surprise,' she said. It was two in the afternoon and she was still wearing a dressing gown. Not that I could say anything about *that*.

'Just thought I'd come and see how you were,' I said. 'I thought you must have had the baby by now.' I glanced down at her tummy. You couldn't really tell.

'He's two weeks old,' she said. 'I had him a bit early.'

We went into the main room of the flat. It had peeling wallpaper, torn curtains, and smelt awful. I took it all in at a glance and felt like running out, but tried to keep a smile on my face.

Gabriel was sitting sucking her thumb and watching the TV blaring out from the corner. I said hello to her but she didn't even look round. There was no sign of the new baby – he was in the bedroom, I supposed.

'What have you called him?' I asked. 'You already knew it was going to be a boy, didn't you?'

'He's called Troy,' Izzy said. 'His dad's Roy, see, so I thought that was quite good.' She snorted, 'Not that we'll ever see his dad.'

'Is he good?' I settled Jack into the crook of my arm, trying not to stare at the dirty nappy rolled up under the chair, or at the three baby bottles with stale milk in them, arranged along the mantelpiece as if they were ornaments.

'He's a little sod. Same as that one was,' she said, pointing at Gabriel. 'I've had to give him more food to keep him quiet. Get him on solids.'

'What d'you mean?'

'I mash a bit of rusk and give it to him before his bottle,' she said. 'It fills him up and knocks him out. Sleeps a treat, he does then.'

'Oh,' I said. 'I didn't know. I didn't think you were supposed to give solid stuff. The books say . . .'

She rummaged down the side of a chair, brought out a packet of cigarettes and lit one. 'What do they know?' she said. 'They don't have to live with it, do they? You need a bit of peace, don't you? You don't have to go by what those books say.'

'I suppose not,' I said, for I'd already sussed that all the mother and baby books took it for granted that you, the mum, had a husband or a partner, drove a car, and lived in a house with a garden. They didn't seem to know there were girls like us.

She nodded towards the other chair, the one with the dirty nappy underneath it. 'Sit down. I'll get you a cup of tea.'

I sat down gingerly. I knew I ought to ask to see the new baby so I could pretend to admire him, but couldn't bring myself to. If this was her sitting room, the room she saw visitors in, what was the bedroom going to be like? I didn't think I wanted to know.

'Look, don't worry about the tea,' I said. 'I'm only passing through.'

Izzy sat down and drew deeply on her cigarette, while I quietly prayed that Jack wouldn't start crying for a bottle. I wasn't going to let him have it here! I didn't want to go into the kitchen and use anything of hers to get it warm, and I didn't want to use her changing mat or her loo or anything else. I didn't even want to put Jack down anywhere. I began to wonder how quickly I could get away.

Izzy dropped some ash into a saucer. 'What you been up to, then?'

'Not a lot,' I said. 'I seem to spend all day doing nothing.'

'That's it, innit?' she said. 'You give your bleedin' life up for them and what thanks do you get?' She nodded towards Gabriel again. 'All she cares about is the telly.'

'I have been out once,' I said. 'I went to *Cascades*. I had quite a good time, actually.' I smiled. 'I met this really nice guy called Mark.'

'Yeah? D'you tell him you had a baby?'

I shook my head. 'It wasn't . . . I didn't talk to him for that long.'

She gave a short laugh. 'You won't talk to him for

long once he knows, either.'

There was a long silence while I struggled to think of something to say. 'Has your mum been round and seen the new baby?' I eventually asked.

Izzy nodded. 'Big deal. She brought me a packet of biscuits.'

I laughed. I felt like crying, though. It was all horrible. Her life was so *miserable*.

I stared down at the greasy carpet and ached to get out of there. I felt that Jack and I might pick up something awful; that I might become like Izzy if I stayed too long.

Jack let out a murmur and I hastily stuck his dummy in his mouth. 'I ought to be getting back,' I said. 'He'll want a feed soon and I haven't brought his bottle or anything.' I waited for Izzy to notice the huge baby travelling bag and ask what was in it, but luckily she didn't. 'You'll have to come and see me next time.'

'Yeah, well, don't hold your breath,' she said. 'I've got *two* to get ready and get out with, remember.'

'Oh well,' I shrugged, getting up and gathering my bits together. 'If you don't turn up I'll pop round here again sometime.'

'Yeah, okay,' she said. 'See yer.'

She closed the door behind me and I thought to myself that it was the most horrible, depressing place I'd ever been and I'd die before I went there again.

I hurried to the bus-stop and the bus came along within a minute. I got on and sat down clutching Jack to me. I'd tell Susie that I'd tried to make a lifeline, but had decided I'd rather drown. So – I didn't fit into the young mums' group, I didn't fit in with my friends and I didn't fit in with Izzy. Where *did* I belong?

I got off, walked to the next bus-stop and looked at my watch. Jack was half an hour late for his feed, but luckily he'd dropped off to sleep again.

I looked up the road to see if the bus was coming and, as I did so, my stomach lurched: *Mark* was coming out of the office building next to the bus-stop. Coming right towards me. I didn't have time to turn away or hide or anything.

And by that time, he'd already seen me.

'Hi!' he said in surprise, coming up. 'What are you doing here? Shouldn't you be at school or college or whatever?'

My heart started beating fast. 'I'm on a course which doesn't start till the end of the month,' I lied. 'I've just been . . . visiting a friend.'

He nodded and leaned sideways and looked at Jack.

The push-chair isn't great for sleeping in, so he'd slipped down and you couldn't see much of him.

'Kid sister?' he asked, and I was just going to tell him, *possibly* I was going to tell him, that no, it was a boy and he was mine, when he added, 'You didn't tell me you had a little sister.'

'Oh yeah,' I said. My heart was hammering and I was nodding like a mechanical dog.

'What's her name?'

'Ellie.' Brilliant lie, I thought. Not even a lie.

'Hmm. Cute,' he said, in the sort of tone which told me he didn't know the first thing about babies and found the whole subject boring.

'Where are you off to?' I asked. At any minute now, I thought, someone was going to come down the road, someone who knew me, and ask me how Jack was.

He patted the camera that was slung round his neck. 'Important assignment for the paper,' he said. 'Life or death.'

'Yeah?' I asked, impressed.

'No,' he said. 'Local flower arrangement class. I have to cover the story and photograph the visiting speaker.'

I giggled. It was a big occasion. I hadn't giggled for ages.

'D'you take photos too, then?' I asked, thinking that it was something to tell Lorna, something to really interest her. 'As well as reporting, I mean.'

'I do the lot, me,' he said. 'Report, photo, type, file, tea-make.' He looked at his watch. 'I've got to go.'

I hesitated, but couldn't, just couldn't, give him my phone number. Funny, that: I was outrageous enough to have a baby but couldn't give a boy my phone number.

'You often at *Cascades?*' I asked instead.

He shrugged. His hair flopped into his eyes. 'Yeah. Sometimes. See you, then.'

'See you,' I said.

We smiled at each other and he went off and I carried on waiting, as if turned to stone at the bus-stop and scared to look round in case he was looking and he suddenly realised and shouted, 'That's *your* baby!'

I bit my lip hard. What had I done now? I should have told him there and then, perfectly casually, that it was my own baby. It was only right at the beginning that I could have done it in an easy, ordinary way.

I'd lied, though. Started a great big lie that I'd have to carry on with.

But maybe I'd never see him again anyway.

17 Maybury Court
Castleton

September 6th

Dear Amy,

Thanks for your letter. I'm glad you're in a muddle as well – but I've just met someone who's worse than both of us put together. I've been to visit this girl who was at my school who's just had her SECOND baby. Her flat was disgustingly horrible. I've been sniffing my clothes since I got in and they smell of her room: chips and smoke and poo. God, I felt really depressed when I came out of there. The worst thing was, she didn't act as if there was anything gross about it at all.

This is only a short letter because my mum asked me to help prepare the meal tonight, so I've got to peel potatoes and stuff. What I'm writing for is to tell you that I went out with my friends the other night and met this boy called Mark. Nothing happened but I really like him. The thing is, I bumped into him today, with the push-chair, but didn't tell him that Jack was mine.

I don't know what to do now. I mean, I might never

see him again but if I do, should I tell him about Jack or keep quiet for the time being? What would you do?

Do you like living at home still or would you like your own place? I thought I wanted my own flat but having seen this one today I don't think I do. I'm not sure if I could cope with Jack on my own, either. My mum drives me mad but at least she knows about things and she can give me a break when she comes in from work. I don't fancy being on my own with Jack for twenty-four hours a day, every day.

I wish there was more room here, though. And that there was a proper garden I could leave Jack in.

It's my birthday in three days' time. I was always going to have a big sixteenth birthday party with a disco and all, but my mum said yesterday that she hopes I'm not expecting anything because she's broke. I'll probably be having a fizzy drink and a biscuit.

Lots of love from Megan

CHAPTER ELEVEN

I settled Jack into the crook of my arm and dialled Claire's number. 'Thanks for your birthday card,' I said when she answered. 'It was really funny.'

'That's okay!' she said. 'Did you get many?'

'Mostly from the family,' I said. 'And my dad had some flowers sent.'

'What did you do on your birthday, then?'

'Nothing, much,' I said, trying to sound as if doing nothing on your sixteenth birthday was quite okay. 'Pushed Jack to the clinic in the morning and tried to make a birthday cake for myself when I came home. It went flat, though. Looked more like a cow pat than a cake.'

'Yeah, well, domestic science never was your thing, was it?'

'So what's it like in the Sixth?' I asked, because they'd been back at school over a week now and she hadn't rung me once.

'It's fantastic!' she screeched, so loudly that it made

Jack jump. 'Really brilliant. I mean, it's not like school at all. The teachers are really nice to us. They treat us like adults and we can call them by their first names!'

I made interested noises. 'So what's Josie doing, then? Doesn't she miss not being there with everyone else?'

'Oh, *she's* all right. God, talk about fallen on her feet: she's got a job in her dad's Insurance office and she's earning *thousands*.'

'Lucky thing,' I said. I was dead pleased that she wasn't in the Sixth with Claire.

'I wouldn't want to be out at work yet, though,' Claire went on. 'I mean, it's a real good laugh at school now. And there's loads of new blokes who've joined from Rivermead.'

'Anyone tasty?' I asked.

'Loads. I've had to do a completely new top ten boys!'

'I bet. Here,' I went on eagerly, 'you remember that boy I met at *Cascades*?'

'The nice one with the floppy hair? Yeah?'

'Well, I *only* saw him last week when I was out with Jack!'

'You didn't! What did you do?'

'Didn't have time to do anything, did I? I just stood

there with the push-chair, trying to look normal.'

'And what happened?' she shrieked. 'What did he say? Did you tell him?!'

'I didn't have to – he thought Jack was my *sister*. I didn't say a thing!'

She gasped. 'Luck-y! But what are you going to do next time. Are you going to tell him?'

'Dunno,' I shrugged. 'That's what I rang for, really. I was wondering if you were going to *Cascades* again. My mum gave me some money for my birthday and I just fancied going out . . . '

'I'm not sure,' she said. 'We haven't got anything arranged.'

I wondered straight away whether that was true or she was just saying it because she didn't want me around any more.

'Some of us from school do things in the evenings together,' she said. 'We go to study centres or watch videos. We had a barbeque last week.'

'Oh, right,' I said, choked. I wanted to go out. More than that I was fairly desperate to see Mark again. I hadn't stopped thinking about him since I'd seen him at the bus-stop. While I was feeding Jack or changing him or doing one of a hundred other dreary tasks, I'd go over everything Mark had ever said to me, trying to work out whether he was interested or was just being friendly.

'We don't just sit around being talked at now,' Claire went on. 'It's not like classes used to be. There's loads of social stuff, it's like team building. And we're all going skiing in January. Thirty of us in a lodge!'

'Fantastic,' I said.

I felt hollow inside. I looked down at Jack's dear little face and of course I loved him, but I still felt hollow inside. I was sixteen and life was happening, but not to me.

Home

September 12th

Dear Dad,

Thanks for the lovely flowers, also for the note saying there's a cheque on its way!

We are fine. I haven't got much news to tell you, except that Jack is getting bigger and bouncier all the time. He's not crying quite as much and – guess what? – he smiled for the first time yesterday. I was stroking his cheek and telling him he was gorgeous and suddenly he gave me this big smile.

It was really funny because I'd just finished talking to my friend Claire and was feeling a bit miserable (only because she seemed to be doing hundreds of exciting things and I wasn't!) and telling Jack all about it, and when he smiled it was like he was trying to make up for everything.

Anyway, it turned out all right because Claire rang me back later and said they'd decided to go out, so I'm going to *Cascades* tonight with her and some of the others. When Ellie comes in from school in a minute I'm going to let her take Jack over so I can start getting ready.

Lots of love, Megan

'There he is!' Claire nudged me. 'He's a bit of all right, isn't he?'

'You're telling me,' I said, giggling. I was having a great time. I was feeling fantastic. I was *out!*

It had all been a bit dodgy at first, because when we'd first got to the club we'd bumped into a group of boys from my school, including some of those who'd been horrible to me when they'd found out I was pregnant. I'd felt sick when I'd seen them, thinking they were going to start something, but all they'd done was just stare at me and snigger childishly. We – all the girls – had just stared back at them hard, and after a while they'd lost interest.

Halfway through the evening Claire, Naomi and I had come out from the dancing part of *Cascades* into the mix-and-mingle bit where the bars were, and Claire had spotted Mark in the bistro area.

I stared across at him and didn't feel half so awkward as I had when I'd seen him at the bus-stop. I was on such a high from being out that I was quite back to my normal, pre-baby and flirty self. While Claire and Naomi went up to the servery to get a burger, I just went straight over to Mark and patted him on the shoulder.

He wheeled round and looked really pleased to see me. 'Hi!'

'Hi, yourself,' I grinned.

'You look as if you're having a good time. How are you?'

'Fine!'

'How's little sis? You looked a bit harassed that day I saw you.'

126

I felt myself going red. 'Oh . . . she's fine, too.'

'Bet your mum's pleased to have you around to take her out, isn't she?'

I nodded and searched my mind for something to change the subject. I wanted to get well off babies before Claire and Naomi came over. I nodded towards the club areas. 'Don't you ever go in and dance?' I asked.

'Tonight? With under eighteens?' He raised his eyebrows. 'Per-lease!'

I grinned. 'Too much fun for you to cope with?'

'Something like that.'

We started talking about the music and so on, finding likes and dislikes we had in common, and then Claire and Naomi came back. I introduced them and they seemed to go from normal to false, tossing their hair back from their faces and, in Naomi's case, speaking to Mark in a husky voice as if she had a cold.

I grinned to myself when I saw them. Too late, I thought. I saw him first.

Somehow, the talk got round to holidays and then to skiing. Claire and Naomi said they'd be going in January and Mark asked why I wasn't going.

'Because I'm on a . . . different course to them,' I said. 'I didn't go into our school's Sixth.'

'Where are you? What course are you taking, then?' Mark asked.

I hesitated and all three of them stared at me, waiting for my reply.

'It's like a . . . a home study course,' I said.

Naomi laughed nervously and I was glad Josie wasn't there to drop me in it.

'I could never study on my own,' Mark said. 'You need real discipline for that. What subjects are you taking?'

'Oh . . . just . . . general subjects,' I said, floundering. 'I haven't made up my mind definitely yet. I . . . I haven't got to decide until the end of the year.'

I could feel myself going tell-tale red again, but luckily someone started a bit of a scuffle in the corner, the bouncers arrived and everyone started looking over and shouting encouragement.

'How did the important assignment go?' I asked Mark when the scufflers had been removed. I turned to Claire and Naomi. 'Last time I saw him he was just going off to report on a flower arranging class for his paper,' I explained.

'Oh, the visiting speaker revealed she favoured winter flowering pansies,' Mark said dryly. 'My editor said they'd never had a scoop like it.'

We laughed and then Claire nudged me. 'Coming back in?' she asked. She looked at her watch, 'We've only got another hour.'

I nodded. I would far rather have stayed there with Mark, but I could hardly do that without being asked.

I smiled at him. 'Oh well,' I said. 'See you.'

'Aren't you going to give him your phone number?' Claire asked, and I gave her an outraged look.

'Go on, you know you want to,' Naomi said, and I gave her one, too.

But really I was pleased.

'Well, aren't you?' Mark teased me.

I got out a piece of paper and scribbled my number on it. 'Here you are,' I said, handing it over. 'Are you going to ring me, then?'

'Probably,' he said. He flung his arm round my shoulders and gave me a matey kind of hug. 'And I can't say fairer than that, can I?'

I didn't say anything, just went back into the club and went *wild* with dancing. It was all going to happen with me and Mark. I knew it was. I was having my best time ever.

And I'd worry about telling him the truth later.

CHAPTER TWELVE

17 Maybury Court
Castleton

September 18th

Dear Luke,

I'm really fed up at the moment. And *tired*. Jack was up three times in the night. He's got a cold and his nose keeps getting blocked up (it's so tiny it takes nothing to block it) and then he can't breathe properly and so can't sleep. Nothing I do stops him whingeing, and then his crying wakes up Mum and Ellie and they moan at me as if it's my fault.

This morning it ended up with me taking him into bed with me and then both of us sitting upright so that his nose would keep clear. Eventually he dropped off and then I was scared to move in case it woke him up again. I was in a really bad mood with him. It's a

131

good job you aren't still living round the corner because if you were, I'd have come round and dumped him on your doorstep.

I can see now why it's best to have TWO parents – so one can take him off sometimes. I tell you, I was pretty close to chucking him out of the window at three o'clock this morning. He's all right at the moment. It's seven o'clock and he's out like a light. (I'm wide awake, of course.)

Anyway, thanks for your letter. Also thanks for sending the cheque from your mum. That was a surprise! If she doesn't want your dad to know she's sent it, I can't really write back to her, so will you thank her for me? I'm going to buy Jack a proper drop-sided cot with the money. He's growing quite tall and is already nearly too big for his carry-cot. He pushes himself right up to the top of it in the night, and then the fluffy hair on his head gets rubbed into a little puff ball. Sweet!

Claire is coming round later and we're going down the high road. It will be just like old times because Josie's not coming. No, it won't really be like old times because we'll have Jack.

Have you met anyone up there? A girl, I mean. You didn't say anything about girls in your letter. You didn't say much at all! And you didn't say anything about Claire, either.

I've met this boy called Mark. He's a bit older than me (twenty) and really nice. He's a photographer and reporter on the *Mercury*. Don't get the wrong idea, nothing's happened – but something might because we get on really well. The thing is, he's had my phone number for *ages* now and he hasn't rung.

I'm not telling you about him to try and make you jealous, I just want to ask you something. If you were going out with a girl and she told you she had a baby, what would you do? Would you think she was easy, or would you run for it or what?

And would you want to know she had a baby right at the beginning, or would you think it was nothing to do with you so you wouldn't think it was any of your business?

You'll guess from this that I haven't told him.

I've sent you one of Ellie's crap photographs of Jack. I'm dying for Lorna to get back from her trip to Italy because she's promised to take some lovely, proper studio-type photos and make him look gorgeous. Not that he isn't gorgeous anyway (but not in the middle of the night). Don't forget to thank your mum.

Love from Megan

It was all very weird – shopping with Claire. We'd done it on Saturdays for ages and ages, yonks and yonks, but we'd never had a baby with us before.

It took hours to get out and I could see Claire was getting fed up with all the last-minute details (another drink, a clean nappy, fresh wipes, change of jacket because of being sick down best one, etc.). Then there was all the business of getting the bus: Jack had gone to sleep by the time we got to the bus-stop and had to be woken up, which he didn't like. When the three of us eventually got settled on a seat an old man went by us, spoke to Jack loudly and poked his tummy and he just *yelled* with fright. Even I was embarrassed at how loudly he screamed, let alone Claire.

Once we were going round the shops, this was different too, of course, because all the cheap trendy clothes' shops we liked going in weren't geared up to having a push-chair dragged through them, and none of their changing rooms was big enough for all three of us. The other thing was, Jack was okay when we were pushing him about but every time we stopped he set up a whinge, so that one of us always had to be pushing the push-chair backwards and forwards to keep the rhythm going and shut him up.

The conversations between me and Claire were all

disjointed, too. I mean, I couldn't ask any meaningful questions, or find out how she felt about Luke, because baby stuff kept getting in the way – like Jack would whimper or let out a sudden yell, or his blanket would fall off and it would distract us.

The other thing was, we didn't pay our usual visit to the travel agent's. Before, pre-Jack, we'd always gone there first to riffle through brochures and look at fares, planning the long stint away from home that we were going on as soon as our mums would let us. We'd had a list of top ten places to visit which changed every week. Now, though, we walked past without even glancing in the window. Claire, I guessed, would be going with Josie or with someone in her precious Sixth if she ever went. And I wouldn't be going at all.

Instead of the travel agent's we went to Boots and Mothercare and Walmans, the up-market department stores.

'Can we go upstairs where the baby stuff is?' I asked Claire, once we'd squirted ourselves with all their perfumes. 'I've got to buy a cot.'

'I thought you were broke,' she said.

I nodded. 'I am – Luke's mum sent me some money, though.'

'Did she?' she exclaimed as we struggled onto the escalator with the push-chair. 'I didn't think they believed that Jack was Luke's baby.'

I shrugged. 'I suppose they do now.'

Claire stared down at Jack. 'He does look like Luke. I can't say why, exactly. He's not even the same colouring. He just does.'

I nodded. 'Sometimes people don't look like other people, but they remind you of them just the same.' We reached the first floor and began to rush Jack through Designer Separates towards the cots. 'It's like . . . Mark reminds me of someone.'

'Yeah, I know – Tom Cruise.'

I grinned. 'Apart from Tom Cruise. I don't know who he looks like – he just reminds me of someone. The first time I saw him I felt that I knew him.'

'Oh yeah? Good one, that.'

'No, *really*,' I said. I smiled dreamily.

'He hasn't rung you yet.'

I shook my head. 'I won't know what to do if he does. I mean, I've *got* to tell him about – ' I nodded towards Jack.

'Yeah. I suppose so,' she said. 'Here, if you were going out with him I bet he'd take you to nice places. He must go into London a lot, working on that newspaper.'

'Oh, I expect I'd be clubbing it and at film pre-mières every night.'

We giggled, and my attention was suddenly caught by a circular stand containing velvet tops: gorgeous soft, stretchy velvet sweaters in rich jewel colours.

We stopped to drool over them. 'Wow!' I said. 'Is my tongue hanging out?'

Claire stroked a particularly gorgeous purple one. 'I'd kill for this,' she said.

We looked at the price: they were nearly a hundred pounds.

'Imagine me, at a film première, wearing this jade green one,' I said longingly. 'Imagine how I'd look.'

'I can't decide between purple and blue . . . '

'Mark would take one look at me and fall madly in love.'

'Yeah. In your dreams.'

I wheeled Jack backwards and forwards to keep him quiet.

'I've got a hundred pounds,' I said suddenly. 'That money I got from Luke's mum!'

Her eyes widened. 'You wouldn't dare!'

'Wouldn't I?' I said recklessly. 'I reckon I deserve a treat.'

She gasped. 'What would your mum say?'

'Dunno,' I shrugged carelessly. 'She was a bit sniffy about the money anyway.'

She had been. She'd said that Luke's mum needn't think she could just send money along and it would be all right, and that if they thought they were going to have a say in Jack's upbringing they had another think coming. But I knew she'd been quite pleased that *she* wasn't going to have to fork out for a cot.

'But what about the cot?'

'What about it?' Now that I had this most beautiful top in the world in my hands, and now that Claire was looking at me with a mixture of awe and disbelief, I didn't care about boring stuff like *cots*. Didn't I need a treat? I'd just had a baby and I'd just had my sixteenth birthday. I deserved this gorgeous thing.

'Jack can stay in his carry-cot a few more weeks,' I said airily. 'It won't hurt him. And I think my dad's going to send me some more money for him soon, anyway.'

Claire stared at the sweaters greedily. 'And they're *classics*, aren't they? If you buy one of these you'll have it forever.'

I nodded. 'It'll be an investment.' I pushed my hands into the pool of sweaters and let them slide through my fingers. I'd never bought anything any-where near as expensive before. I felt quite drunk at the thought of it. 'Now. What colour, d'you think?'

I felt sick by the time I got back to our flats, the tis-sue-wrapped sweater in a glossy carrier bag on the handle of the push-chair. How had I ever done that? How had I paid nearly a hundred pounds for a *jumper?*

When I'd gone up to the snooty woman at the cash desk with it, she'd looked me up and down as if she had a bad smell under her nose, then held each of my notes up to the light, as if they were forgeries. She acted as if someone like me had no right to buy some-thing beautiful.

'Bloody cheek,' Claire had said loudly as we were going down the escalator. 'Your money's as good as anyone's!'

I didn't care about the snobby cow now, though. What was worrying me was what mum was going to say. Should I pretend I'd lost the cot money, should I say that I'd ordered it but it wouldn't be coming for some weeks, or should I just tell her the truth?

Jack was yelling for a bottle as I hurried along the balcony to our flat, so I tried to forget about it for the moment and just rushed in, stuck the kettle on and started getting things ready for his feed.

Mum appeared in the kitchen straight away.

'You've had a phone call,' she said in a strange, accusing voice.

My heart kicked. He'd phoned! I knew it must be Mark – I knew because of the way she'd told me. I pretended not to realise, though. I didn't want her to start.

'Yeah?' I said casually. I got one of Jack's bottles out of the fridge, my hand shaking a bit. He'd *phoned!* A boy of twenty, a good-looking boy with an exciting job, had phoned for me. I wasn't on the scrap heap. My life wasn't all over.

'Someone by the name of Mark.'

'Oh?' I said. *Yeah!* I thought. I poured hot water into a jug to warm Jack's bottle. 'What did he say?'

'He wanted to speak to you.'

'Did you say I'd ring back?'

'No. I didn't. I was very put-out, as a matter at fact. You didn't tell me you had a boyfriend, Megan. After all I've been through with you lately I would have thought . . . '

'He's not my boyfriend!' I protested. 'He's just someone I've met a couple of times. I haven't been out with him or anything.'

'Or *anything?*' she said suspiciously.

'Mum! I haven't even kissed him!'

'Have you told him?'

I settled Jack into a feeding position and looked up at her. 'No. Not yet.'

'Well, you'd better.'

'You didn't say anything about it . . . about Jack, did you?'

'No.' she said. 'But I will if he rings again. So you'd better do it first. You can't expect to keep something like that a secret.'

'I didn't intend to,' I said.

Mum nodded. 'Well, when you've told him, you watch him run for it,' she said. 'You just watch him run.' Her glance fell on the shiny carrier bag amid the cheap polythene ones from Boots and Woollies. 'What's in that nice bag, then? What have you bought from Walmans?'

CHAPTER THIRTEEN

17 Maybury Court
Castleton

September 25th

Dear Lorna,

I haven't heard from you for ages! I know you are really busy. Have you moved on somewhere or are you in the same place?

I found one of your photographs in a Sunday mag. It was a piece on models on holiday and had pictures by various people, and your name was one of the photographers listed. I've cut it out and put it on my wall.

We're fine. Jack's seven weeks old now and getting bigger every day. I expect he'll be sitting up by the time you see him.

If you got my last letter you'll have read about the

boy I met: Mark. I'm still fairly mad about him (well, very mad, actually) but haven't heard from him since he rang here and I wasn't home. Mum spoke to him and I'm sure she was arsy with him and it put him off. I'll probably have to wait now until I go out with Claire and the others and try and see him again. There's one other thing I want to tell you about him: he's more a *photographer* than a reporter. Thought you'd be interested in that.

I did something daft last Saturday. I bought a very expensive jumper – nearly a hundred pounds! Yes, I know it's a lot but it was jade-green velvet and absolutely gorgeous. The thing was, I bought it with the money that Luke's mum had sent to buy a cot, and when I got home with it Mum was UTTERLY HORRIFIED, OUTRAGED and APPALLED (her words).

We had a big row about it, but to be quite honest I'd felt bad about buying it within a minute of leaving the shop. I think I did it to impress Claire more than anything. Anyway, Mum said I had to take it back and I nearly died on the spot: I *hate* taking things back. She dragged me off and (you know Mum) made up some complicated story – something about me having bought it without realising I was allergic to velvet!

The snotty assistant clearly didn't believe a word, so Mum kept going on, saying I used to be allergic to a lot of other things but then I'd had injections, and so on and on and on. I didn't know where to put myself.

Eventually we got the money back, ordered a cot and came home, all without speaking to each other.

It's okay now, though. It has to be, really. If I didn't speak to Mum it would mean I didn't have a proper conversation with a grown-up person ever.

I hope you're not feeling bad at the moment about your adopted baby. I wondered maybe if that was the reason you hadn't written back – because talking about my baby brought everything back and it was painful for you. My social worker, Susie (I don't have to see her any more as a social worker, by the way) said something to me which made me think. I was talking about whether I did the right thing in keeping Jack, and she said there was never any point in anyone regretting their actions, because every one of us acts in the only way we can at that time. I think about this sometimes and it makes sense.

Write when you can.

Lots of love, Megan

I went into town to post Lorna's letter. I didn't need to go that far, of course, but it made a little trip out and trips out were what I liked, because they broke the day up a bit. I was dreading the winter because I knew I wouldn't be able to go out as much.

Carefully avoiding Walmans, I went from the post office to the chemists to load up with the mountain of disposable nappies that Jack got through in a week.

When I was coming out of there I saw Izzy. She didn't see me – I made sure of that. She had a double buggy and was trying to get through one of the swing doors with it. If I'd been nice I would have gone up and helped her, but not feeling nice I turned round and quickly pushed Jack off in the other direction, the haystack of nappies bumping against my legs. I couldn't stop and chat, I thought, because it was nearly time for Jack's next bottle. And I had piles of washing to do. And I had to stand at home looking out of the window. Any excuse. I didn't want to have to talk to her; it was too depressing.

And I was depressed enough. Or, as Mum called it, 'fed up a bit'. Whenever I said I was depressed she said I wasn't, I was just fed up a bit.

I hadn't heard from Claire or anyone. Hadn't got any letters for ages. And, worst of all, hadn't heard from Mark again. Mum had definitely put the boot in for me there.

Being at home all the time, I now fully realised, was awful. More boring than I'd ever thought possible. I often thought about my life with a baby, comparing it to my life without, and the without came out top every time. I never say that in my letters to Lorna, though – in case she thinks I'm regretting keeping Jack. And I'm not. Not really.

It was just so *boring*.

I got home and fed Jack, put him down for a sleep and thought about writing to Dad, but as soon as I got my pad and pen out, Jack woke up again. I winded him, changed him, gave him a few sips of water and put him back to sleep in his new cot, spinning his mobile around to amuse him.

He wouldn't be amused, though, or only for about ten seconds, and then he started crying again. I got him up, looked at his nappy – it was still clean – and tried him with a drop more milk, but he just pushed the bottle away and carried on yelling.

I tried to ignore him and watch TV, but it was impossible. I found my old walkman and put a tape on as loudly as I could without killing my eardrums, but Jack's continual roaring still came through.

I picked him up, put him down and then hung over his cot, asking him what was wrong and nibbling what was left of my nails. I could feel my tummy tightening; I began to feel really angry with him. I asked him to *please* be quiet.

He carried on screaming.

I picked him up again, checked him over, put him down. I had a headache by now and his crying was going right through me. I began to feel that he was screaming deliberately, trying to get me going. He was ruining my life! I had no friends, no boyfriend and no life. All because of him.

I only had him – and he hated me. He hated me because he wanted a proper mum, one who wasn't crap at it. I stared at him resentfully, at his little red, screaming face.

Why wouldn't he *stop?*

I should have given him away, I thought, let him be adopted by someone older, someone who could put up with him and knew what to do with him. I was never going to cope with him. He was going to stop me having a proper life and a proper boyfriend ever again. He was going to stop me having Mark.

'Be quiet!' I suddenly yelled at him. 'Why don't you shut up!'

The screaming seemed to increase in intensity. His legs were drawn up to his tummy, his face was scarlet. He was a little ball of fury.

'Shut *up*, will you!'

I reached into the cot and grasped his shoulders. 'Shut up, shut up, shut up!' I shouted at him, and with every word I shook him.

Suddenly, I realised what I was doing. I dropped him back into the cot, burst into horrified tears and ran out of the room.

Grabbing my jacket from the hall, I let myself out of the flat and slammed the front door behind me. Witches Brew was coming along the balcony and she started to say something, but I just rushed past her and ran down the stairs.

I began to walk very quickly down the road, sobbing, not knowing where I was going and not caring who was looking at me.

I was a hateful, wicked mother. I wasn't fit to have a baby. I couldn't cope. I'd hurt my own baby!

My legs felt shaky. Where was I going? What was I running away from? *Had* I run away? What would happen to Jack if I had? Was he all right? Had I harmed him, shaking him like that? Suppose he had brain damage?

I sobbed harder. *What was I going to do now?*

A green Mini passed me and I suddenly stopped dead.

Susie had a green Mini. Susie, my social worker. Suppose she came along now and saw me? Suppose she stopped and asked me what I was doing and wanted to know where Jack was?

Suppose she found out that I'd left him in the flat on his own?

She'd take him away from me, sure as anything. She'd take him away and give him to someone who really wanted him, someone who could look after him properly and wouldn't pick him up and shake him.

I sat down on the front wall of someone's garden, my eyes blurred with tears.

What was I going to do now?

A woman went by, staring at me. I thought she looked vaguely familiar, but couldn't be bothered to place her.

I started to shake. Suppose Mum came along and saw me sitting on a wall crying? Suppose she found out I'd left Jack on his own? She'd go mad.

I felt ill and desperate and despairing. I was terrified at the thought that Mum or Susie might come along, yet in a way I wanted them to. I wanted them to take over; take charge and tell me what to do.

Tears fell onto my arm. The woman who'd passed had crossed the road and was looking back at me, but I didn't care.

What was I going to do?

There was only one thing *to* do.

I made my hands into hard fists, trying to stop myself crying, then I wiped my face on my jacket sleeve. I stood up and started to retrace my steps home.

Anything could have happened. Mum might have come home early and found Jack screaming himself sick. The flat could have caught fire. Jack could have choked himself crying. He could be dead.

What would I do if I'd caused something terrible to happen to him? What if I'd killed my own baby?

I began to run. The door keys, thank goodness, were in my jacket, and I got them out as I ran. I reached the front door panting, each breath ragged in my throat.

I opened the door. Inside, it was silent.

I ran down the hall and into my bedroom. Jack was asleep. He'd pushed himself up to the top of the cot and was red-faced and damp with sweat. There were traces of tears on his cheeks and every so often his breath caught in a half-sob.

He was all right, though.

I picked him up and burst into tears. 'Sorry . . . sorry . . . sorry,' I said, smothering him with kisses. 'I won't ever *ever* hurt you again.'

He shuddered in his sleep and I gently, carefully, put him back in his cot and covered him up.

CHAPTER FOURTEEN

I spoke to Susie today,' Mum said the following Saturday morning. 'I was asking if there were any educational units round here.'

'There aren't,' I said. 'She's already told me that.'

'No, the nearest is forty miles away. Apparently there aren't enough teenage mums in this area to warrant having one any closer.'

'Pity,' I said.

Mum raised her eyebrows. 'More of a good thing, I should say.'

I was sterilising bottles at the sink and Jack was sitting in his baby seat on the floor, waving a rattle around and dropping it every ten seconds or so.

I hadn't told anyone, not a soul, about what I'd done. I never would. I was going to make it up to Jack by being as good a mum as I possibly could.

But I was still bored out of my skull.

'I suppose forty miles is too far, isn't it.' I said to Mum.

She nodded. 'Apparently you can get an allowance for a taxi to take you about fifteen miles, but that's all.'

I sighed. Jack dropped his rattle for about the millionth time and I bent to pick it up. 'Perhaps I could go to evening classes,' I said lamely. I didn't want to go to evening classes. I didn't even want to go to an educational unit really. What I wanted was to go into the Sixth, with Claire, call teachers by their first names, have interesting lessons and go skiing in January.

I plunged the bottles into the sterilising fluid.

'You must do *something*,' Mum said. 'I don't want you to end up cleaning lavatories for a living.'

Jack threw his rattle and, as I bent to retrieve it, there was a ring at the door.

'I'll go!' Ellie called, and then we heard a moment's conversation and she appeared in the kitchen, looking excited.

'It's a boy!' she said in a gleeful whisper. 'To see you, Megan.'

Mum made a tutting noise.

'What boy?' I said, mystified. 'Is it Luke?'

She shook her head. 'He said to say it was Mark.'

Inside me, I screamed.

Ellie went on, 'When I opened the door he said,

"Oh hello, another sister!" What did he mean?'

'Don't know,' I lied.

Mum looked at me, stony-faced. 'I don't want boys calling here, thank you very much,' she said. 'We've had enough trouble from boys already.'

'It's not like that, Mum!' I said. I turned to Ellie. 'Did you say I was in?'

Ellie nodded. ''Course I did. You are, aren't you?'

I looked down at myself. I was wearing horrible old washed-out jeans with a T-shirt which had baby-sick on the shoulder, and I hadn't even looked at my hair that morning.

And apart from all that, what about Jack?

'Can't you tell him you didn't realise I'd gone out?' I said in a panic.

She looked bewildered. 'How *can* I? I said you were in the kitchen doing the bottles.'

I groaned. Mum drummed her fingers on the table. 'You'll have to go and talk to him, Megan. Explain that it's not convenient to see him at the moment.'

I looked from Mum to Ellie in despair. I'd longed for Mark to get in touch, but not *now*, at this minute – firstly because I looked so revolting and secondly because I hadn't had a chance to explain about Jack. I gave an inward scream: he might hear something right now, while he was standing at the door!

'Go on, Megan,' Mum said. 'Whoever it is, you can't just leave him standing there.'

Slowly, I went out of the kitchen and walked to the front door feeling all hollow and weird. He mustn't find out. Yet he had to . . .

'There you are!' Mark said. He was wearing jeans and a soft blue shirt and looked gorgeous.

'S . . . sorry I was a while,' I said. I dragged a hand through my hair, knowing it was greasy again and that I looked foul.

'I just thought I'd pop in and see how you were,' he said.

'How did you know where I lived?'

'I've just seen your mate.' He gestured down to the other block of flats.

'Claire?' I'd kill her when I saw her.

'I think that's her name. She said you'd probably be in. I rang you once, you know, and then I lost your number.'

I nodded, frozen to the spot, waiting for Ellie to appear and dump Jack in my arms, or Mum to shout, 'Come and take this baby of yours.'

'I haven't seen you around for ages. What have you been up to?'

'Oh, this and . . .' Suddenly, from behind me, there was a screech from Jack. It was the noise he made when he threw his rattle and no one picked it up. I felt myself going red, but Mark didn't seem to notice.

'Haven't been to *Cascades* lately, then?'

I shook my head.

Jack screeched again.

'I've got something to tell you,' I blurted out.

Mark looked at me quizzically.

I swallowed, my mouth dry. 'I can't tell you now. Can I meet you this afternoon? In town?'

He shrugged. 'If you like. Is it important, then?'

I nodded. 'Very important.'

'Okay,' he said. 'See you in that cafe opposite the garage? Bloomers, I think it's called. Three o'clock?'

I nodded, he turned away – and I was just about to shut the door when Witches Brew came bustling along the hallway. She didn't seem to notice Mark as he passed, but when she got to our door she looked back at him and gave me a meaningful wink.

'Here's the cardigan,' she said, thrusting a paper bag at me. 'Hand-knitted and nice and warm. Better than those modern things.'

'Thanks very much,' I said, still reeling from the encounter with Mark.

'Was that your young man?' she asked.

I shook my head. 'Just a friend.'

'Ah, well,' she said. 'Never mind.' She gestured towards the bag. 'Let me know if you want me to knit a pixie hat. Nice for the winter – pixie hats.'

'Yes. Thanks,' I said. I smiled. She was all right, really.

She went off and I shut the door.

Ohmygawd, I thought, as Mum advanced to cross-examine me. I'd actually arranged to meet him. What was going to happen now?

Home

October 1ˢᵗ

Dear Dad,

I've let Ellie take Jack out for a nice long walk and I've just washed my hair and in a minute I'm going out to meet this boy I know.

Thanks for your last letter and I liked the photos. I still haven't got any decent ones of Jack. I'll probably have to wait until Auntie Lorna comes back from Italy before I get any.

We are all well here, although Mum is being a bit funny about things. She keeps telling me she wants me to *do* something, but she doesn't know what. Neither do I. Mum's got the idea that I'm sitting round the house all day just lazing about, while she works all hours to keep us. She has a go at Ellie as well sometimes (she never used to; it used to be just me she went on at). Poor Ellie can't get away from her, either, because they're in the same bedroom now.

Oh well, apart from that everything is okay. Something funny: I've seen this woman around the place a couple of times and thought she was vaguely familiar. Yesterday I saw her again and she seemed to be following me. I thought I must be imagining things but I stopped to look in a window and she came up to me.

She was all in a dither and asked me if I recognised her. I said no, and she said she was Luke's mum! She wanted to see the baby but she hadn't known how I'd react, so she'd been hanging about the flats waiting for a good time to talk to me. People are weird, aren't they?! I remembered seeing her a few days before when I'd been in a right flap, but I hadn't had Jack with me then and she'd been waiting until I had.

I let her take Jack out of his pram and hold him,

and she thought he was gorgeous (she also said he was the image of Luke as a baby, but had my eyes). She asked me to go round to her house one afternoon and I said I would. I haven't told Mum yet, because she was dead funny earlier when Luke's mum sent me some money. The way I look at it, though, it's Mrs Compton's grandchild. Also it will be somewhere for us to go one afternoon!

Okay, Dad, I'm off out now.

Lots of love, Megan

'I'm going out to post this letter to Dad!' I shouted to Mum. I hadn't told her I was meeting Mark because I wasn't up to the GBH of the ear that I knew I'd get.

'Won't be long!' And I bolted out before she could stop me.

I knew Jack would be all right for a couple of hours: Ellie was walking him to the park and then she was allowed (special treat and under Mum's supervision) to give him his next bottle.

I couldn't even think about going to the post office; I was late and anyway I was much too jittery. I stuffed Dad's letter in my pocket and went straight to the cafe. I didn't know what I was going to say, just knew I had to say it.

Mark was already sitting down when I went in, and he had his two cameras and a leather bag on the chair next to him. He said hello, went up to the counter and brought back a coffee which he put in front of me.

'Okay, then,' he said. 'What d'you want to tell me? What's all the mystery?'

I played with the froth on the coffee, trying to work out what to say.

'First your friend Claire was a bit funny about telling me where you lived, and then you couldn't get rid of me quickly enough. What is it – have you got a dad that doesn't like boys coming round or something?'

I shook my head. 'My dad lives in Australia,' I said.

'You've got a fierce guard-dog, then? A fierce mum?'

I managed a smile. 'My mum *is* pretty fierce.' I swallowed. 'No, it's . . . something different. I haven't really been honest with you.'

He shrugged and started laughing. 'It can't be that bad. What – are you an international jewel thief?'

I shook my head. 'It's not exactly about me. Well, it

is . . . ' I carried on messing with the coffee and didn't look at him.

'I've got a baby,' I said in a rush. 'It was him you saw me with a few weeks ago. It wasn't my sister.'

'No!' he said. 'Blimey! A kid.'

'He's two months old and his name's Jack.'

'And where's his father?'

'I don't see him any more. We were going out together last year but we broke up. He's gone to university.'

'Blimey,' he said again.

There was quite a long silence then, during which I drank my coffee. 'Does it matter?' I asked.

'What d'you mean?'

'Does it matter to you that I've got a baby?'

He still looked bemused and I sighed inwardly. How could I put it? I didn't want him to think that I thought that . . .

'Just . . . does it matter to you?'

'Why should it?'

There was another silence. 'I thought – I didn't know if – '

'Look,' he said suddenly, 'I think I know what you're getting at, and I couldn't give a monkey's whether you've got one baby or ten babies.'

'No?'

'Why should I? We're just friends, right? I mean, you're a nice girl I enjoyed chatting to one night. That's all.'

I swallowed hard.

'I mean, where's the problem? Why would I stop being friends with someone just because she had a baby?'

I tried to smile at him but I was choked to bits. *Just friends.* He hadn't come round because he fancied me, he'd come because he'd enjoyed chatting to me and wanted to be friends.

And that was all there was to it.

'I've got a few mates who just happen to be girls. Haven't you got any friends who're boys?' he asked.

I shook my head.

'Look, don't look so put out. It's not because I don't like you. I do! That's why I came round. I just didn't intend having a relationship with you – so whether you're got a baby or not doesn't bother me.'

I nodded, trying to keep a smile on my face.

'You're too young for me, for one thing – my mates have been taking the mick about that. We just seemed to click, though, didn't we? I felt I could have a laugh with you. Know what I mean?'

I nodded again.

'And I guess that might be something to do with having had a baby. You've got more depth to you than most.'

'Right,' I said.

'I'll go and get us another coffee.'

While he was standing up at the counter, I struggled to get things sorted in my head and feel okay about them. It was all right, I told myself. It was better, in a way. Me having a baby didn't bother him, whereas if we were having a proper relationship, it would have done. This way, I had him as a friend. And friends usually lasted longer than boyfriends.

By the time he came back with the coffees, I think I was pretty sorted about it. I still fancied him, of course. That bit wasn't sorted.

'I feel better now I've told you,' I said.

'Good!'

'It's just that I don't know how to handle this sort of thing yet – going out with boys again.' I went red. 'Or not going out with boys.'

'I think you just ought to be honest as soon as possible,' he said. 'You don't have to make an issue of it, just bring the baby into the conversation.'

'Wouldn't you be put off?'

'Not necessarily,' he said. 'Depends if I really liked the girl or not. It might make me like her more.'

'Why's that?'

He looked at his watch. 'Sorry,' he said, 'I'd like to chat but I've got to be at a jumble sale at four o'clock. I've got to take a photo of whoever wins the raffle.'

I looked at the cameras with their long lenses and twiddly bits. 'You don't want someone to practice on, do you? Only I'd love to have some proper photos of the baby – so far I've just got some rubbish ones that my sister took.'

He nodded. 'Sure.'

'Fantastic!' I said. 'My aunt's a photographer too. She was going to take some but she's abroad at the moment.'

'How about tomorrow?'

'Great,' I said. 'If you come early afternoon I'll make sure he's awake.'

A friend was better than nothing, I thought. And a friend who could take photographs was brilliant.

And I'd just have to get over fancying him.

'So where have you been?' Mum asked when I got in and had taken over the running of Jack.

I looked at her to try to judge her mood, and

thought she looked a bit off. I decided not to tell her about Mark until later.

'I told you – to the post office,' I said. Well, I'd been past there, seen the post office.

'Oh yes?' she brought Dad's letter out from behind her back. '*This* was sticking out of your jacket pocket. So you went to the post office, did you?'

I rolled my eyes. 'Okay,' I said, 'I'll tell you where I've been . . .'

CHAPTER FIFTEEN

'Will he take some photos of me with Jack?' Ellie said longingly. 'Oh, will he?'

'I expect so,' I said.

'Will he take some of *me*?' Mum said in an imitation of Ellie.

'I expect so,' I said again. 'If you're good.'

Much to my surprise, Mum had taken the news about Mark brilliantly. In her mind it went without saying that a man of twenty with a good job wouldn't be in the least bit interested in a single mum of sixteen. And as long as he wasn't a potential boyfriend (ie: about to make me pregnant again at any minute) he was all right.

'He wouldn't be bothered with the likes of you,' she'd said. 'I expect he goes out with models and page three girls. Photographers usually do.'

'He's only on the local rag!' I'd said. Nevertheless, she'd insisted on rushing to the shops before they closed and buying Jack a new white towelling stretch-suit to be photographed in, because the ones he'd had since he was born had gone grey with being washed so often.

'You can put him in the new one when you visit Luke's mother,' she'd said. 'I don't want her thinking that we don't keep that baby immaculate.'

I'd nodded. I'd spilt the beans about Mrs Compton the previous day. Mum had been very frosty when I'd first told her, but later she'd decided that having Jack recognised as being Luke's baby was a good thing. 'Then if we have to buy anything major, we can ask them for a contribution towards expenses,' she'd said.

By two o'clock, Jack was fed, watered and glistening with cleanliness. And the three of us had also glammed up a bit. Just in case.

When Mark arrived he had a pile of stuff with him: lights, reflectors and a background screen, as well as his cameras.

I'd been worried about it being embarrassing, but it wasn't. Because he wasn't a boyfriend Mum didn't grill him or anything – and Mark was perfectly okay with me. I reckoned I'd just about avoided making a silly cow of myself. I hadn't flung myself at him saying I couldn't live without him, so there wasn't any awkwardness between us.

Mark propped Jack up on cushions and made him smile and shot off a whole roll of film. He then put him on his tummy, kept clicking his fingers to make him look up, and took another roll, all the time saying what a smashing baby he was, and how cute and good-tempered. After that he did some family shots involving all of us: me with Jack, Ellie with Jack and so on.

He worked quickly and Jack just about lasted out for the time it took, though by the end of the session he'd started giving the irritable squeals that said he was getting tired.

'Ellie and I will take him for a walk in his pram and get him off to sleep,' Mum said. She smiled approvingly at Mark. 'And I think you ought to make this lad a cup of tea, Megan.'

The three of them went off and Mark packed up his stuff and put it in the hall ready to take away.

'I'm really looking forward to seeing the photos,' I said. 'It'll be lovely to have some proper ones to send out. Thanks ever so much for doing them.'

'That's okay,' Mark said. He sprawled at our kitchen table, completely at ease. 'To tell you the truth, it's quite nice to have some different subjects to photograph. It's all good experience. If any shot is really outstanding I can add it to my portfolio.'

I nodded. 'You know I said my aunt's a photographer – she's in the Italian mountains at the moment taking pictures of flowers and mushrooms and stuff.'

Mark nodded, looking impressed.

'She's really good. She's brilliant! I went to stay with her just before I had the baby.'

'Why was that, then?'

'It all got a bit hairy at school. They chucked me out. They said I was a disruptive influence!'

Mark made a dismissive noise. 'That's crazy. I've got a lot of respect for any girl who chooses to keep a baby instead of giving it away.' He hesitated. 'That's what I was about to say yesterday. I'm adopted, see.'

'*Are* you?'

'I never knew my real mother. She didn't want me. She off-loaded me.'

'You sound really bitter.'

He nodded. 'I am.'

'She might not have been able to keep you, though,' I said, thinking of Auntie Lorna. 'She might have really wanted to, but for some reason not been up to it.'

'*You've* managed it. Why couldn't she?'

'Yeah, but I was allowed to come back here to live.

170

Your mum might not have had a proper home to go to or a family to support her. And anyway, it was different in those days.'

'She could have tried it. She gave me up when I was two weeks old. Dumped me!'

'What – on a doorstep or something?'

He shook his head. 'Nah. Not that bad. It amounts to the same thing, though: she chucked me out. Got shot of me.'

'Yes, but . . .' I searched for the words to convince him. 'I bet she went through agony before she did that. I bet she's still going through agony.' I hesitated, 'Look, don't say anything to my mum about this, because she doesn't know, but my auntie – the one I was just talking about – had a baby when she was seventeen. She had it adopted and she told me that she's never, ever, got over it.'

He shrugged.

'She eventually told me all about it because when I was staying with her I was about seven months pregnant, and was thinking about having my baby adopted. She told me that if I went ahead, I'd regret it for the rest of my life. She said that never a day goes by that she doesn't think about her baby and regret giving him up.'

He raised his eyebrows. 'Yeah?'

I nodded. 'And although I wasn't sure what I wanted to do before Jack was born, as soon as I saw him I knew that I couldn't let him go. It was just lucky that Mum came round to the idea, or . . . ' I shrugged, 'I don't know what would have happened: I might have had to give him away.' I bit my lip. 'I can't even *think* of how awful that would have been.'

He didn't say anything.

'Don't you get on with your mum and dad? With the people who adopted you?'

'Sure I do. I get on with them fine. But sometimes I think about the woman who gave me away and think, how *could* you? Why didn't you want me? How could you just chuck me out?'

I shook my head. 'Look, I don't know how she did it, but I do know that it was probably the hardest thing she's ever done.'

There was a long silence. 'Maybe,' he said, and I wasn't sure whether I'd convinced him or not.

We had a cup of tea, and two slices of a sponge cake Ellie had made, and then he said he had to be going. He didn't actually say in so many words, but I got the idea that he was going to meet a girl later on.

'What about getting the photos developed?' I

asked. 'Can I give you something towards the cost?'

He shook his head. 'I can do them at work,' he said. 'We've got a darkroom and everyone brings in their holiday snaps and does them at lunchtimes.'

'Brilliant,' I said, and I thanked him again as I showed him to the door.

He put down his equipment and gave me a brief hug. 'I'll see you later in the week,' he said. 'Friday, probably.'

'Fantastic!' I went back into the flat to sit and wonder where he was going, and who with. I didn't feel *too* anguished, though.

17 Maybury Court
Castleton

October 2nd

Dear Luke,

Thanks for your letter. I'm writing this after being photographed by the local paper!

Well, sort of. You know I told you about a boy I met a while ago in *Cascades?* Well, we got chatting to each other and in the end I told him about Jack. He didn't mind because he wasn't up for that sort of thing anyway. He's twenty and I think he's got a girlfriend of his own age.

Anyway, he's still really nice and he came round this afternoon to take some proper studio-type photos of Jack and all of us. He's getting them developed at work and bringing them back later in the week.

The other exciting thing that happened in the last few days was: me and Jack have met your mum! Have you heard from her? Has she told you already?

I'd seen her around a couple of times but (I think I only met her twice when I was going out with you) didn't realise who she was. Anyway, she came up to me and she was really nice, and she wants me to take Jack round to meet your sisters. She didn't mention your dad! She said Jack was a lovely looking baby with a strong family resemblance to the Comptons. I'm going round to your house when I get the photographs and I'll let her have some.

Nothing else good has happened. I don't see much of Claire, she's got well into life in the Sixth and she seems to be getting over you. I expect you're pleased about this as in your letter you talked about a Japanese girl a lot. Are you going out with her? Don't do anything bloody stupid, like you did with me, will you?

Well, I've got an empty house for the moment because Mum and Ellie have taken Jack out for a walk and I'm going to make the most of it by putting some music on REALLY LOUDLY. I can't do it when Jack is around because he doesn't like the same stuff as I do – he goes all hyper.

Anyway, I'll send you a photo of both of us when I get one. You can leave it on display if you want to frighten off the Japanese girl!

Love from Megan

CHAPTER SIXTEEN

17 Maybury Court
Castleton

October 5th

Dear Amy,

Thanks for your letter and the pic of you and Meredith. I hope to be able to send you one of me and Jack with this. You know I told you about the boy I met – Mark – in my last letter? Well, I've got quite matey with him. It's a pity that's all he is, but it's better than nothing, especially as he's also a photographer and he came round to take photos of Jack last Sunday. He's promised to bring the prints round tonight and I'm going to send you one of those.

How are you coping with everything?

I must say I didn't realise that being on my own at home would be so crap – I've had some dodgy times with Jack crying lately, I can tell you. Sometimes it makes me wonder if I'm really cut out to be a mum. Too late to change my mind now, though . . .

I think next summer will be better as Jack will be older and I'll be able to do more with him. The books say they're better company then. But they also say that's when they get tantrums and throw themselves on the floor and scream. (Something to look forward to.)

I really feel like I want to *do* something: work or study or whatever, but I don't know what. Sometimes I feel that I'm turning into a disposable nappy. I see more of them than I do of people.

This morning I had a really long letter from Lorna – she's more like a friend than an auntie now. I think I told you she was on this assignment in Italy. Well, she's been right up in the mountains – living wild, she said. Anyhow, she's near a town now and she sent me this little suit for Jack. It's really expensive-looking but all embroidered and a bit poncey! I think it's the type of thing that she wanted to put *her* baby in all those years ago.

She talked about her own baby a lot in the letter. I think me having Jack has brought it all back to her. The funny thing is, I named Jack after my dad and she named *her* baby after my dad too (he's her brother). She hadn't told me this before. The difference was, the father of her baby was French, so she called the baby Jacques instead of Jack.

She said that knowing I've kept my baby has made her more determined than ever to find hers, and she's asked me to ask Susie if there's anything else she can do to locate him. If there is, she wants me to start things moving before she gets back. This will be a bit tricky as Lorna is dead against anyone else knowing, so I'd have to do it without my mum finding out. I can't see that it matters after all these years *who* finds out, but Lorna is quite a private person. And I suppose my mum's not the best person to tell those sorts of things.

Give Meredith a kiss for me. Hope to hear from you soon.

Lots of love, Megan

I put Amy's letter to one side to post, and then I went to pick up Jack, who was whingeing in his cot. Balancing him on my hip, I went to phone Claire.

It was Friday afternoon and I really fancied chatting to someone. I knew that Claire sometimes got home from school early on Fridays and I was hoping that she'd ask me over to her place, with or without Jack. I wanted to meet some of these new friends of hers, boys from Rivermead and whoever. I wanted to meet someone who wasn't Jack or Mum or Ellie. And I wanted to tell her about Mark coming round.

Her phone rang and rang but there was no reply. Obviously she was out having a brilliant time somewhere.

Well, I certainly wasn't.

I felt tears of self-pity come into my eyes, longing for something – I didn't quite know what. I just longed for something to happen. Something nice. Often it felt to me as if nothing really nice would ever happen again.

Shifting Jack over to the other arm, I went into my bedroom to change him. We'd go out and post Amy's letter without waiting for the photo, I decided. It would be an outing, and maybe an adventure would happen on the way.

It didn't, though. When we got back, Ellie came in, then Mum, and we all had tea.

Later still I got Jack to bed and made myself look

fairly reasonable for Mark. Oh, I knew he didn't fancy me and he probably never would, but I didn't want him to think I was a dog.

He came round about eight-thirty, bringing the photos. They were absolutely brilliant and Jack looked a darling: cute, cuddly and gorgeous. Mum and Ellie and I spent ages going through them, picking our favourites, and Mark said that we could keep the proof copies and he'd do some special large glossy ones of those we particularly liked.

He was looking at his watch by the time we'd been through the photos for about the tenth time and selected the ones we wanted.

'I'll have to be off,' he said. 'I'm driving to London.'

'Heavy date?' I asked.

'Not really,' he said. 'Just a mate. A girl mate.'

'How old is she?'

'Twenty-three,' he said, and I nearly died. Twenty-three! That was practically as old as Mum. It just went to show that he'd *never* be interested in me.

I went with him to the door and he said he'd come back soon and bring the enlargements.

'It might be nice if I came round and took regular photos of Jack,' he said. 'You'll have a record through the years, then.'

'Oh, that would be *great!*' I said. 'Brilliant.' If you could.'

'Yeah, I'd like to,' Mark said. 'He's a smashing kid. Right little Jack the lad, eh?' He grinned, 'Funnily enough, I was nearly called that myself.'

'What – Jack?' I said, surprised.

'Almost. I was called Jacques when I was born, but then my adoptive parents re-named me.'

'What?' I nearly passed out. I literally had to hold onto the open door to steady myself. '*What?!*'

'I was called Jacques when I was born,' he repeated, looking at me strangely, 'but it was a bit too French and fancy for my new mum and dad.'

I couldn't speak. Just couldn't speak.

'They re-named me Mark Daniel,' he went on. 'I suppose they just wanted to put their own Mark on me. Ha ha!'

I couldn't smile. I could do nothing but stare at him.

Could it *really* be?

Oh, of course! That's why he looked familiar, why I felt as if I knew him. He had Lorna's thick dark hair and her slanty eyes. He had her straight nose. They were the same type of person . . . they were both photographers.

'How – how old are you exactly?' I asked in a wobbly voice.

'Twenty-one in December,' he said. 'Why?'

'N-nothing,' I said. I was shaking all over by now.

'Will you come back next week?' I said. 'I want to – I – ' I dried up. I couldn't tell him. It wasn't my secret to tell. Lorna would have to tell him herself.

He nodded, looking at me bemused. 'I said I would. Soon as I get the prints done, okay?'

'Okay.'

He patted my cheek with his free hand and I watched him go to the end of the walkway, and then I went into my bedroom feeling delirious and hysterical and completely out of it.

I paced up and down, hugging myself, trying to think things through. So this boy I'd fancied, this boy I'd felt I had some link with, I actually *did* have a link with. He was my cousin. He was my cousin as well as my friend. He wasn't going to be my boyfriend, but he'd probably be the sort who'd stick by me and be there for me whatever.

And what about *Auntie Lorna?*

She'd supported me and helped me so much when I was pregnant. There couldn't be any better present in the world, any more fantastic way of repaying her

183

than finding her long-lost baby. How was I going to tell her, though? What would she *do?*

And how was I going to tell Mark? Should I go on a bit more first about how sorry Lorna was . . . about how much she'd longed to find her baby? Should Lorna really be the one to tell him?

I'd have to think about it carefully. I could ask Susie, and maybe I'd have to tell Mum, too, and see what she thought.

I gave a little shriek of happiness. However it was told, it was the most fantastic, wonderful thing ever!

And the other brilliant thing was discovering that nice things could still happen. *Did* still happen.

So maybe, if I pushed on and didn't give up, I could make more nice things happen. I could find a way of taking those blasted exams. I could get on, get going again, re-start my life.

I let out another little squeal and – I must have been delirious – picked up Jack even though he was sleeping soundly. Holding him to me, I began to dance round the room with him.

Poor little thing, I thought – having me for a mum. Being woken in the night to get up and dance. But he was smiling and making a tight, chuckly noise. He was *laughing*.

'What's up with you?' Ellie said, coming in and looking at me as if I was mad. 'Why have you woken up Jack and why are you dancing?'

'I don't know!' I said.

'What?'

I didn't know if I could tell her, I meant. I ought to let Lorna know first – but I didn't know if I could possibly keep the news to myself for another half-second.

'I'll be in there in a minute,' I said. And then I'd decide what to do. But there was something else I had to do, first. 'Can you take Jack for me?'

Pulling a bewildered *What's up with her?* face, Ellie took Jack and went out.

I got out my writing pad.

Dear Lorna,

I've got something to tell you. It's the most exciting thing in the world so I hope you're sitting down.

I'VE FOUND YOUR BABY.

Ring me immediately you get this and I'll tell you everything.

All my love, Megan

If you have enjoyed this title, why not try something else ...
  full of the mysteries of the harem ...

taking you to the edge of endurance ...

DIANE MATCHECK

THE SACRIFICE

about boyfriends, sisters, and sisters' boyfriends ...

That Summer

S a r a h   D e s s e n